SHE
DIDN'T
DIE

D.L. SLETTEN

She Didn't Die
D. L. Sletten

This is a work of fiction. Names, characters, places, and incidents are either the product of the author's imagination or are used fictitiously, and any resemblance to any actual persons, living or dead, events, or locales is entirely coincidental.

All rights reserved.

ISBN-13: 978-1-941212-81-3

Cover Designer: Deborah Bradseth

SHE DIDN'T DIE

PROLOGUE

Twenty Years Ago

"Aaron. I really don't want to go there," Cassandra Sanders said, staring at the inky black sky on the deserted country road. "You know I don't like your friends. Let's turn around and go to the all-night graduation party instead."

Aaron Jackson smiled reassuringly at Cassie. "We'll stop there for a few minutes and then head to the grad party. I promise."

Aaron turned left onto a dirt road that was lined with tall pines. The road was even darker here, despite turning on the brights on his Ford F-150 pick-up. The truck bumped and bounced as it made its way toward a lighted cabin in the distance.

Cassie shivered despite the warm weather. She grabbed Aaron's letter jacket and slipped it on. "I hate his place. I don't know why you guys like to come here. It's in the middle of nowhere."

"Ah, you know how Jason is. He likes having his blow-out parties out here in the woods. And high school graduation is a big deal," Aaron said. "He just wanted one more big bash before summer began, and we all leave for college in the fall."

"And you're sure there'll be other girls there too?" Cassie asked. "When we've come here before, I was the only girl. I hate being alone with your friends. They creep me out."

"Jason said they invited a lot of other people," Aaron assured her. "Don't worry. We'll have one beer and leave." He glanced over at Cassie and smiled at how cute she looked wearing his letter jacket. They'd been neighbors their whole life and had gone to school together since kindergarten. She was one of the prettiest girls in their small-town school with her long blond hair and big blue eyes. She also had the perfect figure, as far as he was concerned. Unfortunately, Cassie only saw him as a friend and not a boyfriend. He wished she liked him the same way he liked her.

They came to a clearing, and Aaron pulled the truck next to a line of other trucks and cars. His was older and beat up compared to his friends' cars, but he didn't care. He was just happy to have his own wheels. His parents weren't as rich as his friends' parents, and Aaron had to work to buy his own truck. But he didn't mind, even when the other guys razzed him about his old truck.

Cassie looked around. "I just see your friends' cars. No one else is here."

"I'm sure the guys brought friends along in their cars. Let's go in." Aaron jumped out of the driver's side and ran around to help Cassie out of the truck. She was wearing the same summer dress and heels she wore to graduation, and he didn't want her hopping out onto the gravel and getting hurt.

Still wearing Aaron's jacket, Cassie and Aaron approached the cabin door. The old hunting cabin was set in the middle of one hundred acres of thick forest with the Morgan River skirting it. It was prime land for deer hunting and Jason and his father and cousins used it every November. There was no electricity, so it was lit inside by oil lamps, and there was a stone fireplace in the main room.

Aaron opened the door and walked inside. His friends, Jason, Marty, Tony, and Craig were sitting on the old sofa and chairs, drinking cans of beer.

"Hey! You made it. I almost thought you'd chickened out," Jason said, standing up. He was much shorter than Aaron and stockier. His thick brown hair was cut short, and his brown eyes were so dark they were nearly black.

"Where is everyone?" Aaron asked, glancing around. He felt Cassie move closer to him.

"Everyone is here," Jason said, grinning.

Marty grabbed two beer cans and handed them to Aaron and Cassie. He wasn't much taller than Jason and was pudgy despite having played football and basketball over the past four years with the other guys.

Aaron opened his beer, but Cassie set hers down on an old, scratched end table.

"Everyone drink up! The guest of honor is here!" Jason said, downing the rest of his beer.

Aaron frowned, his eyes darting around. "What do you mean by that?"

Jason grinned. "You know what I mean. We do this every year when school's finished. At least every year since the tenth grade."

Fear gripped Aaron. He placed his arm around Cassie and held on tightly. "You said this would be a graduation party. I thought you were through with that other stuff."

"Well, I lied." Jason laughed and walked toward Cassie, but she stepped back and Aaron did also. "Now, now. We'll have none of this," Jason said, reaching for Cassie and pulling her away from Aaron. "You are our reward for graduating high school. And we're going to enjoy every minute of it."

"Aaron!" Cassie yelled in a high-pitched voice filled with fear. Her eyes darted around the room as if looking for an escape route.

Aaron stepped toward Jason. "No! Not Cassie. You leave her alone."

Jason laughed. "Like you could do anything about it. Boys. Show Aaron out."

The other guys walked toward Aaron, looking deadly serious. Aaron was tall and strong, but there was no way he could fight all three of them. He backed up toward the door but stood firm.

"Jason! Why? The other two girls weren't even from around here. Why would you want to do this to Cassie? To me?"

Jason instructed Marty and Tony to take hold of Cassie, then walked up to Aaron. "Because she's the ultimate prize. The head cheerleader and prom queen. The prettiest girl in school. Why wouldn't I want to have her as my reward?" He laughed. "Besides. She was never yours. Cassie never would have let you touch a hair on her head, let alone have sex with her. Now, she belongs to us."

Aaron's heart pounded as he watched fear fill Cassie's eyes. Tony and Marty held her tightly as Craig moved furniture out of the way to make room on the old rug.

Jason moved closer to Aaron, shoving a finger in his face. "And don't even think about running for help. You were there when we buried the other two girls. You're in this as deep as we are. And you brought us the greatest prize of all. Try proving you weren't involved."

"I never touched the other girls. You can't blame anything on me," Aaron yelled.

"No? Well, try snitching and see. Besides, my father, the Sheriff, will cover this up so quickly your head will spin, and you'll be left holding the blame. Now," Jason walked over to where Cassie was being held by the other boys. "Either join us or leave," Jason told Aaron. He grinned. "Wouldn't you like a piece of this?" Jason pulled a knife out of his pocket, snapped it open, slid it into the bodice of Cassie's dress, and cut it all the way down to her waist. Cassie gasped as Aaron stood against the door, feeling helpless.

"Please," Aaron begged, tears burning in his eyes. "Please stop. I'll do anything if you just leave her alone."

The other guys laughed as Jason turned toward Aaron. "I don't want anything from you. I have what I want. Now go. Leave!"

Aaron looked at Cassie as her eyes pleaded with him to help her. "I'm sorry," he said, tears spilling down his cheeks. "I'm so sorry." He ran out the door to his truck. The last thing he heard was Cassie screaming his name.

* * *

Aaron spun out his truck, and his back tires spewed dirt as he drove recklessly down the road to the highway. Tears clouded his view, and his head pounded. Cassie. His beautiful Cassie. Why had he brought her here? Why had he been so stupid to think Jason wouldn't try to hurt her like he'd hurt the other girls?

He stomped on his breaks and sat in the cab, struggling to think of a way to save Cassie. He couldn't let himself imagine what the guys were doing to her right now. It was all a nightmare. But he couldn't fight them all. And Jason was right. Jason's father was the country sheriff, Marty's father was the mayor, and Tony's father was the district attorney. Craig's father was the superintendent of schools but was also on the city council and was tight with the other fathers. If Aaron went to the authorities for help, they'd all cover it up or blame him for hurting Cassie.

What could he do?

Wiping his eyes, he drove slowly down the road. When he came to another rough road on the left, he turned and drove down it. This road took him to the back of the cabin, where Jason's father had built a shed to hang dead deer to drain the blood before they butchered them. Aaron turned off his headlights and backed up to the shed. From here, he could see the light through the cabin's back window.

As Aaron sat there, he thought about the course of events that brought him to this moment. He'd always been a good kid; quiet, polite, and respectful. He and his older sister never gave their parents a reason to worry. All through grade school, he and Cassie had been friends, even when the boys teased him about playing with a girl. It wasn't until middle school that Aaron's athletic abilities began to shine, and he was accepted by Jason and his group of friends. Now, he wondered why he'd been so intent on being friends with them at all.

"Think!" he yelled into the cab, and it echoed back at him. If he ran to town for help or even to the other town twenty miles away, his life would be ruined. His father, who was an engineer for the county, would probably lose his job. His mother would be heartbroken that Aaron was involved in such a vile act. Everyone's life would be ruined—all because he was so stupid.

"Think!" Aaron had to do something. But what?

Suddenly, he remembered what was locked inside his glove compartment. He grabbed the flashlight he kept in his cab and unlocked the compartment. A .22 caliber semi-automatic handgun sat in its holster. Aaron pulled it out and snapped off the magazine to check if there was any ammo left. The gun had been a gift from his parents for his eighteenth birthday. He and Jason had been out target practicing with it just the other day, and that's why it was still in his truck.

There were ten rounds left in the magazine.

Aaron stared at the cabin. He could run there right now and kill them all to save Cassie.

But what if he missed? With only ten rounds, he might not get them all. Or worse, what if he accidentally shot Cassie? No matter what he did, he was screwed. He could run for help and end up in jail for life or kill them all and land in jail. Aaron dropped his head in defeat.

Dark thoughts crept into his mind. He had one other choice. He could end his suffering right now.

Aaron snapped off the safety and placed the barrel to the side of his head. All he had to do was squeeze the trigger, and all his anguish would be over. Cassie was going to die tonight, so why shouldn't he?

Sweat dripped down his temple as he held the gun to it. His hands turned clammy. *Just pull the trigger,* he thought. *End it all now!*

Aaron took a deep breath, then dropped the gun to his side. Coward! He was a coward. He couldn't save Cassie, and he couldn't even kill himself. He was useless.

The sound of car engines starting and tires on the dirt road made him open his eyes. The guys were leaving. Aaron looked up and frowned. He saw flames through the small back window. He jumped out of his truck and smelled gasoline and smoke. Christ! They'd set the cabin on fire.

And Cassie was in there.

Aaron took off in a sprint toward the cabin.

CHAPTER ONE

Twenty Years Later

Deputy Aaron Jackson walked into the Morgan Falls Sheriff's Department and nodded to the front desk clerk, Rhonda Jorgensen. It was a typical September day in the small town of Morgan Falls, Minnesota. The leaves were beginning to change color, the children were all tucked safely in school, and the nearly 12,000 residents were going about their daily business. Not much happened in this small town, and Aaron liked it that way.

Deputy Kevin Dudley, the oldest officer on staff, glanced up from his paperwork as Aaron sat at his own desk.

"How's it going this morning?" Duds asked.

"Good." Aaron smiled. "Quiet and peaceful, the way I like it."

Deputy Dudley nodded. "Just a few more months, and I'll be out of here for good, fishing every day. Let's keep things quiet and calm until then."

Aaron laughed. "I don't blame you. But nothing exciting ever happens in this town."

Sheriff Jason Hughes poked his round head out of his office.

"Aaron. I need to talk to you."

Aaron sighed and stood, heading to the Sheriff's office. At thirty-eight, Aaron was still slender and in good shape. He played basketball at the high school gym with some old school buddies twice a week and tried to run at least three mornings a week to stay fit. As he entered Sheriff Hughes' office and shut the door behind him, he thought his old friend from high school could use a few laps around the track. Jason Hughes had gained a lot of weight over the years and didn't seem to care.

Sheriff Hughes sat behind his desk, leaned back, and put his feet up. "I thought you might want to be saved from Duds going on about fishing." He grinned. That same evil grin he'd had since high school. The same grin that made Aaron's blood boil every time he saw it.

"I don't mind Duds talking about retirement. He's worked hard all his life, so he deserves it," Aaron said. He remained standing, hoping to leave the office quickly.

"My old man would be retiring soon if he hadn't keeled over and died three years ago," Hughes said. "Thank God! I'd still be just a deputy if he were still alive."

Aaron winced. "I liked your dad. He hired me right out of college. He was a good sheriff, and he was always fair with me."

Hughes scoffed. "Don't remind me. He hired you over his own son. But I won in the end. I ended up being sheriff after all."

Jason's father had hired Aaron over Jason years ago and finally hired his son when he thought Jason was more mature. But Aaron knew better. Jason was still the conniving jerk he'd been in high school. If Aaron hadn't already had several years in the department by the time Jason became sheriff, he would have left.

"Anything else you want?" Aaron asked, itching to get out

of there. "I need to get out on my rounds."

"I hear old lady Sanders died this morning," Sheriff Hughes said. "I wonder what will happen to her house and stuff since her husband has already passed."

Aaron didn't even blink. "I suppose her daughter will sell the house and other things."

Hughes scoffed. "Cassie is long dead."

"Apparently not," Aaron said smugly. "She was with her mother these past few days after her stroke. She was sitting with her this morning when she died."

Hughes' feet hit the floor, and he stood up. He was several inches shorter than Aaron and not intimidating at all. "What are you talking about? Cassie is dead."

"No, she's not. My sister works as an RN at the hospital, and she told me it was Cassie. We lived next door to them our whole lives, so she should know. Plus," Aaron paused a moment, enjoying the look of terror on Hughes' face. "You know I still live next door to their house since I bought the house from my mother. I've seen Cassie coming and going this past week. She's older, just like we are, but it's her."

Hughes stared at him, his face blank. He really hadn't changed much since high school except for in size. Jason still had a buzz cut and his eyes were still nearly black. Aaron was enjoying Jason's stunned silence.

"Wait. You knew Cassie was here, and you didn't tell me?" Hughes said, staring daggers at Aaron.

Aaron shrugged. "Why would I tell you? She's here to bury her mother and sell the house, and then she'll be gone again."

Hughes glared at him. "Have you talked to her?"

"Me? Talk to her?" Aaron laughed. "I'm the last person Cassie would want to talk to besides you. I've left her alone, as

I expect you and the other guys should, too."

Hughes dropped into his chair. "You should have told me she was here. If it is her."

"It's her," Aaron said.

"I always wondered why she wasn't reported missing," Hughes said. "Her parents never said a word about her. She was just gone."

"Lucky you." Aaron glared at him.

Hughes' eyes darted up. "How did she survive the fire? That cabin and everything in it was nothing but ashes."

"How would I know. I wasn't there," Aaron said.

Hughes narrowed his eyes. "You don't seem bothered by the fact she's in town. You're just as guilty as the rest of us. You brought her to the cabin."

"I was tricked into bringing her there," Aaron shot back. "You lied to me. So no, I'm not bothered at all that Cassie is home. But maybe you should be."

"She can't do anything after all these years," Hughes said. "It's too late to press charges, and there's no evidence other than her word against ours."

Aaron shrugged. "If you think so."

"I want you to follow her. Make sure she doesn't talk to anyone or start anything, you hear?" Hughes said.

Aaron laughed. "I can't stop her from talking to people. It's a free country, last I heard." He turned to open the door.

"That's a direct order, Deputy Jackson. Keep an eye on her. Follow her if you have to. I don't want her here any longer than she needs to be."

Aaron stood with his hand clutching the doorknob. "Yes, Sir," he said tightly. Then he swung open the door and strode out of the building.

* * *

Aaron wasn't going to follow Cassie around town. That was ridiculous. He planned on leaving her alone to grieve her mother and take care of her personal business. Jason couldn't fire him without a good reason—and following a woman who Jason tried to kill wasn't a reason he'd want to put down on paper for all to see.

Instead, Aaron made his usual rounds. He drove up and down the streets of their small town. He helped an elderly man whose car had stalled on the highway, and he picked up lunch for his now elderly first-grade teacher, Mrs. Haines, who he knew was housebound and enjoyed a special meal every once in a while. This was his town. He knew a great many people who lived here and had known them his entire life. People liked and trusted him. He wasn't going to tarnish his image by tailing a woman who'd been brutalized by teenagers two decades ago.

At lunchtime, Aaron turned into his driveway and parked his service vehicle. He preferred making a quick lunch at home to eating fast food. As he walked up the three steps to the front door, he noticed a car pulling into the driveway of the house next door. For an instant, he thought about turning and waving to Cassie, then decided against it. So, he hurried inside to make a sandwich from the roast he'd cooked the night before.

Aaron had never planned on staying in Morgan Falls, let alone working as a peace officer. After high school, he'd gone to the University of North Dakota in Fargo to attend college. His goal was to become a lawyer. He took criminal justice classes and by the end of his four years, had somehow changed his mind to become a police officer. About the same time that he graduated, his parents told him about the opening at the sheriff's department in town. Aaron went home for the summer and applied; certain he wouldn't get it because Jason had applied also. But Aaron did get the job, and after working for a few months with Jason's father, he'd decided to stay. Arthur Hughes was not the same as his son. He was honest and cared about the community. During that time, Aaron's father was killed in a car accident, and two years later, his mother remarried and moved away. So, he ended up in his childhood home because he could afford it and working with the one person he hated the most—Jason.

After eating his sandwich, Aaron headed back outside to get into his car. He noticed that Cassie's car was gone. He figured she was running around making arrangements for her mother's funeral. That made him sad. He'd always liked Cassie's parents, and they'd always been nice to him while he was growing up. But, ever since that dreadful night, they had ignored Aaron whenever they saw him. Aaron didn't know if Cassie had told them what really happened, but it seemed they knew something and possibly blamed him.

The guilt of that night constantly weighed on him.

Aaron drove slowly around the neighborhood to make sure all was well. He circled the grade school and middle school, then made his way through the more affluent neighborhood on the northern side of town. His other three "friends" lived there. Tony, Craig, and Marty. Tony Wiles had become a lawyer like his father and was now the district attorney for the county. Craig Becker was the fire chief in town. His father had been the superintendent of schools, but Craig wasn't one for college. He'd trained to be a firefighter and eventually moved up to the coveted position of chief.

Marty Kroger had followed in his father's footsteps and become the mayor. Everyone thought he was as nice and personable as his father had been, but Aaron knew it was all a show. Heck, even Marty's wife had given up on him. Marty had gotten heavier with age and drank incessantly. After twelve years of marriage, his wife had left Marty six months ago. So now Marty lived alone in the biggest, nicest house in town and drank up his profits from the liquor store he'd inherited from his father.

"What a waste!" Aaron said aloud as he drove past Marty's house, then circled the cul-de-sac and headed back past it. As he drove by, a woman hurried out the front door of Marty's house and headed for her car at the curb. Aaron was stunned. What on earth was Cassie doing inside Marty's house?

CHAPTER TWO

Cassandra Sanders was exhausted. She'd been sitting with her mother night and day since she received the phone call that her mother had a stroke. She'd flown there immediately and had been with her mother ever since. The doctors told her that her mother, Christine, had a brain bleed that wasn't operable, and so the waiting began. From the moment Cassie arrived, her mother was comatose, and she never had a chance to say goodbye.

Cassie sighed as she walked into her mother's house that morning after Christine passed. Cassie no longer thought of this house as her home, even though she'd grown up in it. And she never told anyone other than close friends and family that she was from Morgan Falls, Minnesota. After that dreadful night, Cassie never wanted to see this place again. But since her parents had no choice but to stay and live out their lives there, she did come back when it was absolutely necessary.

Cassie was hungry, but she was too tired to make anything from the slim pickings in the kitchen. Mrs. Orton, who lived next door, had brought her a hot dish to heat up along with a pan of brownies. So far, she was the only person who'd acknowledged that Cassie was here. Cassie hadn't shown her face in town for twenty years, and the people she used to know probably didn't even remember her. Except for Mrs. Orton and Amy Jackson, now Cranston, who worked as a nurse in the hospital. Amy had grown up next door to Cassie and recognized her immediately. The only other person who'd probably recognized her was Aaron, Amy's brother. But Cassie didn't want anything to do with him.

Cassie needed a few hours of sleep, and then the work would begin. She had to plan her mother's funeral and then go through everything in the house and get it ready to sell. Lying down on the sofa, she texted her husband, James, in California to tell him her mother had died. He'd wanted to come with her and help, but Cassie had declined his offer. She hated this town and the people in it and didn't want to expose her husband to this place. It was better for her to just do the work alone and put Morgan Falls far behind her.

After sleeping for a couple of hours, Cassie showered and dressed. She needed to run around town and do some errands. She drove to the funeral home first to make sure they'd received her mother's body from the hospital. Then she picked out a nice casket and made the other arrangements. Her mother had already purchased a plot next to Cassie's father, who'd died two years ago of a heart attack. They picked a time and date, and Cassie said she'd write up an obituary that evening and get it to them the next day.

Feeling drained and hungry, she decided to give Mrs. Orton's hot dish a try. She was also craving one of the neighbor's frosted brownies. As Cassie turned into her mother's driveway, she froze. Aaron Jackson, her one-time best friend and long-time neighbor, was just walking up the steps of his front porch. She parked the car and sat still. The last thing Cassie wanted was to talk to Aaron. She was surprised that she hadn't run into him before this in the week she'd been there.

Cassie watched as Aaron stopped a moment and glanced her way. Her heart pounded. *Don't you dare walk up to me,* she thought. Then, he turned and went inside, closing the door. Cassie let out a breath that she hadn't realized she'd been holding in and relaxed. She wished her parents' house had an attached garage so she'd never be seen coming and going. Unfortunately, the garage was detached, and also filled with stuff.

Getting out, she hurried to the side door that opened into the kitchen and locked the door behind her. Cassie wasn't afraid of anyone in this town, but by habit, she always locked her doors. She definitely wasn't afraid of Aaron, but she would feel uncomfortable around him. It would be best if they stayed away from each other while she was here.

The hot dish was actually very good, so Cassie decided she'd reheat it for dinner, too, since there was so much of it. The brownie was heavenly. It was the first real meal Cassie had eaten since coming back here. At the hospital, she'd mainly eaten food from the vending machines. The nurses offered her her mother's hospital meals since they came with the cost of the room, and Cassie had accepted them a couple of times. But mostly, she hadn't been hungry as she watched her mother slowly fade away.

After eating, Cassie found her bag with her supplies and summoned her courage. She had a few house calls to make to people she didn't like or trust. But she had to do it. There was something she needed to know, and if it meant talking to the people she despised, then so be it.

Cassie pulled out of her driveway and headed toward the north side of town. As she drove down the quiet street, she was surprised by how nice and new these homes were. Growing up in Morgan Falls, everyone lived in an old farmhouse or homes built in the forties or fifties. The town had flourished after WWII because of the papermill built there. But in the eighties, the papermill closed, and all the good-paying jobs disappeared. So, she was surprised that people here made enough money to build these nice homes.

Glancing at her phone, she found the house she was looking for. Martin Kroger. Now, the town mayor, just as his father had been. Cassie cringed inwardly as she parked at the curb in front of his house. It was amazing what a person could find on the internet these days. Finding Marty's address had been simple. She, however, didn't have a footprint online. Cassie was careful not to be on social media and didn't hand out her information readily. She never wanted to be as easily found as Marty was.

Looking around and not seeing anyone, Cassie grabbed her bag and stepped out of her car. Happy she'd worn jeans and sneakers so she could move quickly, Cassie hurried up the sidewalk, then knocked on the door.

After a time, the front door opened, and a hefty, medium-height man wearing a robe answered. Cassie studied him for a moment to make sure it was Marty. He didn't look well, and from the smell of alcohol wafting off him, he was also drunk.

"Do you remember me?" she asked him.

Marty frowned and stared at her, then his eyes grew wide. "No! You're dead." He backed away and tried to shut the door, but Cassie stepped into the frame and put her hand on the door to keep it open.

"I'm not dead. Surprise."

Marty began shaking.

"Don't have a heart attack for crying out loud," Cassie said. She was trained as a trauma nurse and worked in an emergency room, but the last thing she wanted to do was save the life of one of her attackers. "Listen. I just need you to do something for me," she said quickly before he passed out from fear. "It's simple and quick."

Marty shook his head. "No. You're dead. I helped start the fire," he said.

"Marty! Stop it! All I'm asking is a simple thing, and then I'll leave. You owe me at least that," Cassie said.

Marty stood there a moment, then seemed to calm down. He nodded. "Okay. Come in."

Cassie walked inside and shut the door.

CHAPTER THREE

That evening, Aaron was sitting at his desk finishing paperwork when Sheriff Hughes strode out of his office.

"You coming to the city council meeting tonight?" Hughes asked, staring at Aaron. "They're planning the yearly budget, and I want to make sure they plan for us to keep on a third deputy after Duds retires."

Aaron sighed. He had hoped to go home and settle in front of the television while eating dinner. Watching a mindless show sounded much better than listening to the mayor and council members talk all night.

"Yeah, sure. I'll be there. Six o'clock, right?" Aaron asked. "I'll grab something to eat and be there."

"Good." Hughes walked closer to Aaron. They were the only ones in the room except for Deputy Frank Sorenson, who was getting ready to do his evening rounds.

"Did you watch her today?" Hughes asked quietly.

"No. I didn't follow her around all day," Aaron told him. "I saw her around town while I was doing my rounds. Nothing odd about that. She's planning a funeral, after all."

Hughes' eyes turned to slits. "Well, keep an eye on her. I mean it. Shouldn't be hard since you're right next door." He turned and headed back into his office.

Aaron stood, grabbed his brown uniform jacket, and headed out of the building. He hated greasy burgers, but that's all he had time for tonight.

At six forty-five, Aaron showed up at the city hall council chambers and sat at the back of the room. A few of the councilmen and women were already there, sitting in their assigned seats. Several residents of the small town were also there, but not as many as there should be. Everyone complained when their property taxes went up for necessary services, but no one ever wanted to sit through a budget meeting to find out why. Honestly, Aaron didn't want to either.

Sheriff Hughes sauntered in, saw Aaron, and headed straight for him. "Have you seen Marty? He's not here yet, and he's not answering his phone."

This piqued Aaron's interest. "I haven't seen him in a few days. He's been holing himself up at his house since his wife left him."

Hughes' face wrinkled in disgust. "Yeah. And he's been drinking like a fish these last six months. Disgusting. I'm glad I never got married."

Aaron stared at him. "Lucky you."

Craig Becker walked in and gravitated toward Hughes and Aaron. "Hey, guys. You must be worried about your budget, too. I swear, they cut our budget every year and then wonder why we don't have enough people to man the station."

Craig was still in fairly good shape and if he'd been a nice guy, his blond, blue-eyed looks would have attracted every available woman in town. But everyone knew he was bossy and mean. His fire crew hated him, and his wife left him two years ago and took the children with her. Aaron had felt sorry for Craig's wife. He knew she'd put up with a lot of abuse from Craig. The guy was as big a jerk now as he was in high school. Some people never changed.

"Have you seen Marty today?" Hughes asked Craig. "He hasn't shown up yet."

Craig laughed. "He's probably already three sheets to the wind by now."

Anthony Wiles walked in at that moment. As district attorney, he didn't have a reason to attend the meetings, but he liked checking out the women who came. Tony was known for his wandering eye despite having been married for years. Everyone knew he and his wife were close to divorce because Tony had slept with nearly every bar waitress in town.

"Why are you here?" Hughes asked Tony. "You aren't required to attend."

"Neither are you, but here you are," Tony shot back. "I pay property taxes. I like knowing where my money goes. Especially since my wife owns that good-for-nothing gift shop that loses money every year."

Aaron rolled his eyes. Rich people's problems.

Hughes glanced up to where the council members sat. There was an empty chair in the middle where Marty was supposed to be. "This is ridiculous." He pulled out his phone and called Deputy Sorenson. "Frank. Go by the mayor's house and pound on the door until he answers. He's late for his own meeting." He clicked off the phone.

The four men moved up to sit in the second row. The rest of the people sat down, too, as the council members shifted nervously in their seats, eager to get started. Finally, Hughes' phone rang.

"What?" he said brusquely.

"Ah, Sheriff? I think you'd better come to the mayor's house. And bring backup." Frank's voice sounded shaky.

Sheriff Hughes stood. "Why? What's wrong?"

"The mayor is dead."

* * *

Sheriff Hughes, Aaron, Tony, and Craig all arrived at Marty's house at the same time. Behind them, they heard the ambulance and fire truck sirens. Deputy Sorenson was bent over on the front lawn, losing his dinner in the flower beds.

"What's happening?" Sheriff Hughes shouted.

Sorenson wiped his mouth with the back of his hand and stood up. "He's inside," he said shakily.

Hughes led the parade of men toward the front door with Aaron right behind him. They crowded into the expansive entryway, and all looked up at once.

"Jesus Christ!" Sheriff Hughes bellowed.

Marty hung from a noose from the top railing. His eyes bulged from their sockets, and his tongue was hanging out. His body circled slowly around and around like some kind of creepy dance. The only clothing he wore was an open robe.

Tony blanched and ran out to join Frank in the flower beds. Craig stared up in stunned silence. Aaron was the first one to come to his senses.

"We have to cut him down," Aaron said, taking the curved staircase two steps at a time.

"Wait!" the sheriff yelled. "Shouldn't we wait until the paramedics come?"

Aaron glared at him. "Paramedics aren't going to do a thing

for Marty now. Do you want someone to take a picture of him like this?"

Sheriff Hughes finally came to his senses. He hurried up the staircase behind Aaron. "We can't just cut him down and let him fall all the way to the floor."

Aaron and Hughes stood on the landing next to where the rope had been tied to the railing.

"Maybe we could pull him back up here," Aaron suggested.

Hughes stared at him. "He's at least three hundred and fifty pounds!"

"Just do it!" Aaron shouted.

The two men grabbed ahold of the rope and pulled. It was slow going. Once the body was close to the railing, they were both sweating.

"Craig! Get up here and help!" Hughes called out.

Craig came out of his stupor and ran upstairs. Between the three of them, they were able to drop Marty's body onto the landing. By this time, the paramedics had arrived and climbed the stairs.

"You aren't supposed to move the body," Joe, the paramedic, said, staring down at Marty's unmoving figure.

Sheriff Hughes glared at him. "He was dead already. I doubt if moving him was going to do more harm."

Joe shrugged. "You'll have to explain that to the coroner."

While they waited for Calvin Evans, the county coroner, to arrive, Hughes pulled the men outside to speak privately.

"Why would Marty kill himself?" the sheriff asked. Tony, Craig, and Aaron stood with him in a circle.

"Because his wife left him. Because he has no children to carry on his name. Because his liquor store is going belly-up. Because he drinks too much and made a terrible decision,"

Aaron said. "Just to name a few reasons."

Hughes glared at him. "He was our friend. How can you be so flippant?"

"I'm not being flippant. But everything I said is true. Maybe he couldn't live with himself any longer."

"He has been depressed," Tony piped up. "The other day, he said he might as well be dead because he didn't care anymore."

"Really?" Hughes asked, looking surprised. "He's never said anything like that to me."

"That's because you don't listen to people. You talk over them," Tony said acidly.

"It could be because she's back," Craig whispered.

Aaron's blood boiled. He knew exactly who "she" was. "Cassie had nothing to do with this," he said. "More than likely, his guilt got to him."

Sheriff Hughes' eyes widened. "Could she have killed him?"

Aaron rolled his eyes. "Jesus, Jason. She couldn't be more than one hundred and thirty pounds soaking wet. How on earth could she make a man his size jump from the balcony with a rope around his neck?"

"I don't know," Hughes said. "But there has to be a good reason why Marty hung himself, and I'm going to find out what it was."

Tony frowned. "Cassie's back? How can that be? She's dead."

"No, she's not," Hughes said. "She's very much alive, and she's here in town for her mother's funeral."

"Why didn't anyone tell me?" Tony asked angrily. "Shit. I could have run into her in town and thought I was seeing a ghost."

"I only told Jason," Aaron said. He turned to Craig. "How

did you know Cassie was back?"

"I saw her," Craig said, still whispering. "I thought I was seeing things. Then someone told me Mrs. Sanders died, and her daughter was here to make arrangements. How can she be alive? We left her on the floor. We covered everything in gasoline. We..."

"Shut up, you idiot!" Hughes growled. "Do you want everyone to hear? She survived somehow, so deal with it. Let's just hope she leaves town as soon as she's done with everything."

The coroner arrived and looked everything over before telling the paramedics to bag the body and take it to the morgue. By then, a big crowd had gathered around the house. Since Deputy Sorenson still looked pale, Sheriff Hughes told him to go home. Only Aaron and Hughes were left at the scene. Tony and Craig had left, and so had the rest of the fire crew.

"So, what do you think?" Hughes asked Calvin.

"I think he's dead," Calvin said.

Hughes crossed his arms over his wide chest. "But did he hang himself, or was he murdered?"

Calvin looked surprised. "Were you expecting him to be murdered?"

"I'm just asking your professional opinion," Hughes said impatiently.

"Well then, you'll have to wait until I've had a chance to do the autopsy. I can't give you answers until then," Calvin said. He nodded and left. The only people left on the scene were Hughes and Aaron.

"I'm going home. It's been a long day, and I'm beat." Aaron walked toward his car.

"Hey! We still have to look around the house for evidence and notify his ex-wife," Hughes said to Aaron's retreating back.

"Not tonight. Lock it up, and if the coroner says there's something fishy, we'll investigate. And you get the privilege of calling Mrs. Kroger." Aaron opened his car door.

"Me! Why me?" Hughes asked.

"Because you make the big bucks," Aaron said. He slid into his car and drove home. As he drove, he only had one thing on his mind. Why had Cassie been in Marty's house that afternoon? And did she have anything to do with his death?

CHAPTER FOUR

Aaron had trouble falling asleep that night. He kept seeing Marty's bloated face and bulging eyes. Death was not pretty—especially a death by hanging. He'd only come upon one other suicide in his career, and that had been a farmer ten miles out of town who'd blown his head off when he learned the bank was repossessing his property. It had been a grisly sight, but since he'd been a stranger to Aaron, it hadn't bothered him as much. Seeing Marty, however, was different. Even though they weren't close friends anymore, he was still someone he'd known all his life. That made it more chilling.

Finally, at six a.m., Aaron got up, put on shorts and a sweatshirt, and went out into the quiet streets to run. Running always helped clear his mind and made him feel better. He ran through the neighborhoods, past the old papermill on the river, and back around town to his house. When he passed the bakery at the edge of downtown, he couldn't resist the smell of fresh pastries. He bought two donuts and two apple turnovers and, clutching the bag, ran the rest of the way home.

He was running up his driveway at eight-thirty when he

saw Cassie walking to her car. Aaron made the decision to risk saying hello.

"Hi, Cassie," he called as he ran in her direction. He stopped a few feet away from her and noticed her eyes narrow as she stepped back. "I just wanted to tell you how sorry I am about your mother. I always liked both of your parents, and I'll miss her not living next door to me."

Cassie stared at him as if he were an alien. She was still the prettiest girl—woman—he'd ever seen with her shoulder-length blond hair, expressive blue eyes, and shapely figure. She'd hardly changed in twenty years.

"Am I supposed to pretend this is a happy reunion?" Cassie said venomously.

Aaron was taken aback by the hatred in her voice. "Um, no. I mean. Well." He didn't know how to respond. "I just wanted you to know I was sorry."

"You have a lot to be sorry for," Cassie said. She turned and opened her car door.

"Marty died yesterday," Aaron blurted out. He didn't know what made him say it.

Cassie turned back toward him. "Do you really think I care? After what he and all of you did to me, I hope you all drop dead." She slipped into her car, started it, and squealed out of the driveway and down the street.

Aaron was left standing there, stunned.

* * *

After showering and dressing, Aaron showed up at work at ten. The office was buzzing. Rhonda was answering a barrage of phone calls, and so was Deputy Sorenson. Deputy Dudley seemed dazed by all the disruption going on, and Sheriff Hughes was locked in his office.

"What's happening?" Aaron asked Duds. "This can't be from what happened last night."

Duds shook his head and turned to Aaron. "It's been crazy here. People are calling asking what happened to the mayor. They want the sheriff to have a press conference to tell everyone what's going on. But Sheriff Hughes refuses to say anything until the autopsy is complete. Newspapers and news stations from all over the state and even from Fargo are calling. I've never seen so much commotion."

Aaron was stunned. Why was everyone interested in the suicide of a small-town mayor?

"Deputy Jackson! Come to my office," Sheriff Hughes bellowed out his open door.

Aaron sighed as all eyes turned to him. He stood and walked into Hughes' office. Hughes was already pacing in front of his desk.

"Close the door," Hughes said.

Aaron shut the door and stood there, waiting for Hughes to speak.

"This town is going crazy," Hughes said. "Somehow, the news of Marty's death has spread, and everyone wants to know if it was suicide or if we have a murderer on the loose." He stopped pacing and stared at Aaron.

"What do you think?" Aaron asked.

"It's not what I think. It's what I know," Hughes said cryptically. He went behind his desk and sat down, pointing to the chair near Aaron. "Sit."

Aaron hated being spoken to like a dog but sat down anyway.

"The coroner came up with a preliminary report," Hughes said. "He won't have the toxicology for a while, but he knows what happened to Marty."

"What?" Aaron sat forward in his chair.

"He was strangled."

Aaron frowned. "Uh, yeah. He had a rope around his neck."

"No," Hughes said, sounding annoyed. "He was strangled and then hung from the banister after he was already dead."

"That's ridiculous. Why would someone strangle him and then hang him? Why make it look like suicide?"

"Because she didn't want it to look like murder," Hughes said.

"She? You're not trying to tell me that Cassie strangled Marty and then lifted his three-hundred-and-fifty-pound body over the railing, are you?" Aaron said. "Because that is ridiculous."

Hughes glared at him. "Who else would want Marty dead?"

"His soon-to-be ex-wife. Someone angry about the rise in property taxes. Someone who works at his liquor store. Christ, Jason. I'm sure there are a number of people who hated Marty enough to kill him," Aaron said.

Hughes studied him for a moment. "Why are you so quick to defend her?"

"Why are you so quick to blame her?" Aaron asked. "She's been quiet all these years and is only here to bury her mother. Leave her alone. She isn't hurting anyone."

"I want you to continue keeping an eye on her," Hughes said. "And I want you to ask her where she was yesterday. This is now a murder investigation, and as far as I'm concerned, she's the prime suspect."

Aaron stood. "Fine. I'll talk to her, but don't you dare go

near her. She nearly had a heart attack when I said hello this morning. We are the last people on earth she wants to see, with due cause."

"Just follow her. Craig is scared out of his mind and Tony isn't all that happy either. Just make sure she stays away from them," Hughes said.

Aaron nodded, spun around, and left the office, shutting the door harder than necessary. As he headed for his service car, he wasn't sure if he was mad at Jason or at himself. After all, he had seen Cassie leave Marty's house yesterday afternoon, and he'd kept it to himself. But why was she there? And could she really have murdered him?

Aaron drove his usual route around town as he contemplated how to approach Cassie. He helped a little girl find her cat, which had climbed up a tree. He told a homeless man to move on from a spot in the woods near a nice neighborhood. He gave him twenty dollars to get a meal and a card for the closest homeless shelter one town over. Then he parked his car and walked around downtown, checking on the businesses to make sure all was well. It was then that he saw Cassie's car parked in front of the florist shop.

He stood outside for a moment, wondering if she'd be more open to talking to him in a public place. Taking a breath, he walked inside Hadley Flowers and Gifts.

The bell chimed over the door as Aaron entered. The place smelled like roses and carnations and was filled with stately antique furniture and tables that displayed floral arrangements and gifts for sale.

"Hey, Aaron. I'll be right with you," Jenny Hadley said from behind the counter. She and Aaron had gone to high school together, and she now ran her parents' shop. That was typical of a small town. Kids who stayed ended up working for their parents.

Aaron waved back and then saw Cassie. She'd been off to the side of the counter, paying Hadley, most likely for flowers for her mother's casket. Cassie glared at him.

Aaron walked around, pretending to be interested in the displays until Cassie strode in his direction.

"Are you following me?" she demanded.

Her sheer anger made him take a step back. "No. Not at all. I was doing my rounds downtown."

"Like I believe that," Cassie said.

"Since you're here, I'd like to ask you a couple of questions," he said. "About Marty's death."

Her brows shot up. "What? You think I killed him?"

"Uh, no. I don't. But it's now become a murder investigation, and I was told to talk to you," Aaron said.

Cassie's eyes narrowed.

"Hey, Aaron. Can I help you with anything?" Jenny came up to them with a big smile on her face.

Cassie turned to leave, and Aaron spoke quickly. "No, thank you, Jenny. Have a great day." He rushed after Cassie and caught her outside beside her car.

"I just need to ask you a few questions. That's all," Aaron said.

"Ask, but then leave me alone."

"Have you seen Marty since you came back to town?" Aaron asked, already knowing the answer.

"Why would I? Why would I go and chat with one of my rapists?" Cassie hissed.

Aaron drew closer and spoke quietly. "Cassie. I saw you leaving Marty's house yesterday afternoon. I haven't told anyone yet. What were you doing there?"

Cassie waited a beat before answering. "It's nobody's business why I was there. But he was very much alive and drunk when I left. Honestly, Aaron. Do you really think I'm strong enough to kill someone that large?"

Aaron shook his head. "No. I don't."

"Then there's your answer." Cassie slid behind the wheel of her car and rolled down her window. "Why don't you go back to your disgusting sheriff and tell him that. I can't believe that after all these years, you're still his lackey. You both disgust me."

Aaron stepped away from the car as she pulled out of the parking space and drove away.

Later, back at the station, Sheriff Hughes waved for Aaron to come into his office.

Lackey, Aaron thought. *She's right. I'm still following Jason's orders.*

"Well? Did you talk to Cassie?" Hughes asked once Aaron was inside, and the door was shut.

"Yes. I did. Cassie didn't have anything to do with Marty's death. And she was insulted that I would even ask," Aaron said.

"Maybe I should bring her in for questioning," Hughes said.

Aaron stepped forward, placed his hands on Jason's desk, and put his face close to his. "Leave her alone! Remember. If you push her too far, you're putting yourself at risk."

Hughes pulled back. "At risk for what? Her killing me?"

Aaron stood upright and laughed. "You'd wish she'd killed you instead of what she could do. She went to the hospital in the neighboring county that night. She had a rape kit done. All she'd have to do is point a finger and your DNA will expose what you and the others did. So, leave her alone."

Hughes' eyes grew wide in his round face. "How the hell do you know that? Did she threaten us?"

"I know a lot more than you think," Aaron said. "It doesn't take a brain surgeon to look up cases in other counties. At the time, she said a group of boys she didn't know grabbed her outside the grad party and raped her. She didn't identify any of you then, but she could now. So, if I were you, I'd back off."

Hughes sat back, contemplating this new information. "You got this info online?"

"It's easy enough to find. It's in the police reports."

"Hm. So that's why she never had us arrested." His eyes darted to Aaron. "But that doesn't explain how she escaped the fire to begin with."

"Who knows? You were stupid enough to not kill her. She must have come to and crawled out. I noticed a scar from a bad burn on her inner arm."

"Or maybe you helped her get out," Hughes said, his dark beady eyes boring into him.

"I wasn't there, remember?" Aaron spat out. "And I certainly didn't hang around to watch what you did to my best friend."

"Fine," Hughes said, his chair creaking as he sat back. "I'm having a press conference tomorrow at nine a.m. Everyone in town is freaking out about Marty's death. I expect you to be there, backing me up. As far as any of us know, someone strangled Marty and left him hanging to make it look like a suicide. The investigation is ongoing."

"Have you investigated his house for clues?" Aaron asked.

"A forensic team is coming up from Minneapolis tomorrow to go over everything thoroughly. So, it's basically wait and see." Hughes sat up again. "I also talked to the soon-to-be ex-Mrs.

Kroger. She's in St. Augustine on a girls' week with friends. And she lives in Minneapolis now. She hasn't seen Marty in months."

"She could have hired someone to kill him," Aaron offered. "If she's still on his life insurance policy, she'd make out well."

Hughes shrugged. "Could have, but I doubt it. His wife went to college to become a librarian and volunteered all over town while they were married. I doubt if she's cold-hearted enough to have him killed. But it's something to look into."

"I'm going home," Aaron said, turning to leave. "I'll see you tomorrow."

"Nine o'clock sharp!" Sheriff Hughes yelled at his back.

Aaron waved to Duds as he walked out the door. Dudley liked working the late evening shift so he could fish early in the morning before work.

Aaron slipped into his personal car and headed home. As he drove through the darkened streets, he decided to pull through Marty's cul-de-sac just to make sure the house was undisturbed. With all the attention this case was getting, he wouldn't put it past photographers to try to get into the empty house.

Aaron slowly drove his car past Marty's house and noted that all was well. He passed Tony's house, then Craig's, made the circle, and headed back down the street. As he came near Tony's house again, he saw a woman hurrying out his front door and heading to a car at the curb. Aaron's headlights shined on the woman, and he recognized her immediately. It was Cassie.

CHAPTER FIVE

Cassie was unnerved after talking to Aaron for the second time that day. It was bad enough he'd spoken to her this morning, but then he'd followed her into the flower shop and approached her again. What was wrong with him? How could he not understand that she didn't want to talk to him?

After driving away, Cassie was so upset that she decided to go to the little diner downtown to have lunch and calm down. Since she'd been in town, she'd only seen a couple of people she'd known from high school, other than Aaron. At the hospital, Amy had recognized her, and then at the flower shop Jenny had given her a warm welcome home. Calling this place home always made Cassie bristle, but since no one in town other than the men involved knew what happened to her here, everyone else assumed she was happy to be back in Morgan Falls.

Cassie walked into the small-town diner and found a booth in the back. As she passed a few tables, some of the people smiled at her, and others waved. She was surprised anyone remembered her at all. She hadn't been in town for decades, other than to bury her father two years ago. Her parents used to come to visit her in California once a year and were there when she married sixteen years ago. But then again, people in small towns always seem to remember everyone no matter how old they get.

The waitress came over with a menu and a stout glass of water. "Hey, Cassie! I'd heard you were in town. Remember me? We were in cheerleading together."

Cassie stared at the tall, chubby woman with short black hair standing in front of her. Her name tag said Sandy. It finally hit her who she was, and she smiled. "Hi, Sandy. It's been a long time."

Sandy smiled. "It has. I can no longer do the splits or a backflip, and I have two kids in high school." She laughed. "How have you been?"

"Fine," Cassie said. She didn't want to tell too much about herself. "I work as a trauma nurse in California, and I'm married. And I can't do the splits either." She smiled.

"Wow. A nurse. That's great," Sandy said. "I never had a chance to go to college. Was married right out of high school, and the two kids came pretty quickly. You remember Billy Waters, don't you? That's who I married."

"Nice," Cassie said. "I remember him being a cutie in high school."

Sandy smiled widely. "He's still a cutie. He works construction."

"That's great." Cassie wasn't surprised. Most guys around here either farmed or worked construction. Both were good-paying jobs if you worked hard.

"What can I get you to drink?" Sandy asked.

Cassie asked for a diet Coke and ordered a BLT sandwich without bothering to look at the menu.

After Sandy left, she scanned the restaurant to see if there was anyone else there from her high school years. Not seeing anyone, she pulled out her phone and texted her husband, James. She'd met James while she was working nights at a hospital in San Diego. She'd been working there a year, and he was doing his residency. It took her a long time to trust men again, and James was the first person she'd become serious with since high school. He'd been kind and sensitive, and after she'd opened up to him about her brutal attack, he'd been even more careful not to push her. That eventually made her love him more.

Sandy came back with her drink and then stood there a moment. Cassie looked up to see what she wanted.

"Did you hear about Marty Kroger's death?" Sandy asked in a hushed voice. "I hear he hung himself."

Cassie's brows rose. Hung himself? She hadn't heard that. "Sounds awful," she told Sandy.

"I bet it was. Frank Sorenson, he's a deputy, found him. I guess he took it pretty badly. Sheesh, he's just a kid, like twenty-four years old." Sandy shook her head. "You know, I never really liked Marty. He gave me the willies in high school. That whole crowd he hung out with did. Especially Jason, who's now our sheriff. How on earth he managed to be elected to that position is beyond me. I suppose everyone thought he would be like his old man."

Cassie just nodded. The last thing she wanted to do was talk about those guys. But it was interesting to hear that Sandy hadn't liked them in high school, too.

"Oh. Your sandwich is ready. I'll be right back," Sandy said, rushing off.

The place became busy after that, so Cassie didn't have

to worry about Sandy gossiping with her anymore. But she couldn't get the picture of Marty swinging from the end of a rope out of her mind. It gave her chills.

She left a big tip for Sandy and waved to her on her way out of the diner. As she neared the door, she saw Tony Wiles sitting at the counter, flirting with a very young waitress wearing a low-cut top. Tony turned and saw Cassie, and his face turned pale.

Cassie stared at him a moment longer than was polite, then turned and left. *Let him shake in his boots,* she thought. He was next on her list.

Cassie drove home and waited until sunset.

CHAPTER SIX

Aaron awoke at seven the next morning, surprised he'd slept at all. Seeing Cassie leaving Tony's house the night before had weighed heavily on him. Since he'd been driving his own car, she hadn't even looked up as he passed. What had she been doing there?

He went to the kitchen and started a cup of coffee on his Keurig. While he waited, he stared out the window toward Cassie's house. Other than an occasional coat of fresh paint, neither house had changed much since he was a child. Cassie's house had always been painted white with black trim, even when her father repainted it a few years ago. There was no fence between the yards—never had been—and as kids, they'd run back and forth between their backyards playing on Cassie's swing set or in Aaron's sandbox. In the summer, Mrs. Sanders filled a rubber pool full of water, and they splashed and played in it, screeching over the icy water. In the winter, they built snow forts and had snowball fights. So many memories, now tarnished because they were no longer friends. Because of that night.

"Because I was stupid," Aaron said aloud to the empty room, shaking his head.

He took his coffee into his bedroom and headed for the shower. When he bought the house from his mother, he'd spent vacations and weekends remodeling it. He'd opened up the master bedroom to twice its size by knocking out a wall to the other bedroom, and he'd added a bathroom. He'd finished off the basement with a bedroom and bathroom and a game room for a pool table. While the outside still looked the same, the inside was new and updated.

Unfortunately, he had no wife or children to enjoy it with.

As Aaron showered, he thought again about seeing Cassie come out of Tony's house. After she'd driven off, he'd returned to Tony's house and studied it. Should he go inside and ask Tony what Cassie wanted? Should he check on him? If he did that, it would mean he believed Jason's theory that Cassie had killed Marty. So, instead, Aaron had driven home. But he hadn't slept well, thinking about what he'd seen.

Once dressed, Aaron drove to the station. He waved to Rhonda, who looked frazzled from all the calls coming in, and then went over to where Frank sat.

"Ready for this one-man show?" Aaron asked.

Frank looked confused for a moment until he figured it out. "Yeah. We're just supposed to stand there and keep our mouths shut."

Aaron chuckled. "You got that right."

Finally, at eight-fifty-five, Sheriff Hughes strode out of his office and waved for them to follow. The three officers walked outside to the front of the building, where a microphone was placed. A few eager photographers and hungry journalists stood a few feet away from the podium. There was even a news van from Fargo. Aaron, Frank, and Hughes took their places behind the podium, and the news conference began.

Afterward, Aaron followed Frank and Hughes back into the office.

"I'm glad that's over, for now," Hughes said. "I hate taking questions that I can't answer."

"What time is the forensic team coming?" Aaron asked.

"They should be here by ten," Hughes said. "I'll meet them at the house and let them in."

The sheriff turned to go into his office while Aaron and Frank moved toward their desks. Before anyone could sit down, Rhonda rushed over to them, her face pale.

"What is it?" Aaron asked, suspecting something terrible must have happened.

"I just had a call from Jackie Wiles. Anthony Wiles is dead."

* * *

Aaron drove Hughes to the scene in his own service vehicle with Frank right behind them.

"What the hell is happening?" Hughes kept saying over and over again. "What the hell is happening?"

"We'll figure it out," Aaron said gently, afraid Hughes was going to have a nervous breakdown. First Marty, now Tony. Two deaths weren't a coincidence.

The paramedics had already arrived at the house by the time they parked their car and so had Craig Becker.

"What's happening?" Craig asked, looking shaky. That seemed to be the question of the day.

"We don't know yet," Aaron told him. "Stay out here, and we'll go inside and talk to Tony's wife."

Tony lived in a house nearly as big as Marty's. It was a two-story with a finished basement. The main floor had a kitchen, family room, dining room, formal living room, and an office. Since it had been built in the 1970s, it wasn't an open floor concept. Every room was separate.

Aaron and Hughes entered the house and looked around. The entryway wasn't as grand as Marty's house, but there was a staircase that went up to the second floor and then a hallway that led to the kitchen. The formal living room was to the left, and the office was behind closed doors to the right. They both knew the layout of the house from having attended parties there.

Jackie Wiles sat in the blue living room on the left, crying on the shoulder of their fifteen-year-old son, Matt, who looked stunned. Another female sat with them, offering coffee, tea, or anything else to help.

"Tea isn't going to fix this," Hughes said sharply to Aaron. "But I guess it's nice she's trying."

Aaron shook his head in disgust. Just when Aaron thought Jason was semi-human, he made an inappropriate comment like this and reminded him that Jason was a jerk.

The office door opened and out walked the paramedic, Joe. "He's dead all right," he told Hughes. "Gun to the head. We didn't touch anything until you've had a look."

A female paramedic, Claire, followed Joe outside. Aaron didn't know her well, but he thought she looked queasy from what she'd just witnessed.

"Let's go in," Hughes said, heaving a heavy sigh. He led the way and Aaron steeled himself for a gory scene. They both stopped across the desk from the victim. Aaron's stomach lurched. The left side of Tony's head was blown off.

Aaron tried to stop his breakfast from coming up. He studied the scene. Tony sat in his chair, still dressed in his clothes from yesterday, leaning to his left side. Both arms hung straight down at his sides. His desk looked fine, everything stacked neatly and in its place. Except for the blood and possibly pieces of his brain on the desk, floor, and books in the bookcase behind him, all looked well.

"Here's the gun," Hughes said, pointing to the floor on Tony's right side. "He must have dropped it after he shot himself."

Aaron frowned. Something was off, but he wasn't sure what it was.

"It clearly looks like suicide," Hughes said, coming around the desk again. "But why? Tony was always so cocky and sure of himself. What would make him want to kill himself?"

Aaron thought for a moment. "You said the gun is on his right side?"

"Yeah. Why?" Hughes asked impatiently.

"So, he shot himself in the right temple?" Aaron said.

"Are you blind? Look at him. Yes, he shot himself in the right temple," Hughes said angrily.

Aaron turned to Hughes. "Tony was left-handed."

Hughes stood there for a moment, letting this information sink in. "Shit."

They decided to leave everything as it was and let the forensic team that was working at Marty's house come here and look over the scene. The coroner arrived, too, and pronounced Tony dead.

"No shit, Sherlock," Hughes said.

Calvin glared at him. "I have to officially pronounce him dead before you can start the investigation. So don't be such a prick."

"Will you do an autopsy?" Aaron asked, trying to keep Hughes quiet.

"Why? It's clearly a suicide. Let's see what the team from the cities think before we decide that," Calvin said. "Have the body sent to my office if an autopsy is necessary." He left.

Aaron sighed. "Shut the door so Jackie and Matt can't see inside. This had to be devastating for her to find."

They closed the door and Hughes put in a call to the forensic team leader who was just down the street. After the call, he nudged his head in Jackie's direction. "Let's go talk to her and the boy and see what they know."

Aaron and Hughes both gave their condolences to Jackie and Matt, then asked the friend if she'd get them coffee while they talked to the family. Once they were all sitting down, Hughes asked Jackie if she'd heard anything the night before.

Jackie shook her head. "I was out with friends at the casino, playing bingo," she said. "I didn't get home until eleven and never heard anything after that."

Hughes frowned. "Weren't you worried when Tony didn't come to bed?"

Jackie looked down at her lap as she twisted a tissue in her hands. She was a petite brunette who worked hard at Pilates and yoga to maintain her figure. "Tony and I have separate bedrooms. I had no idea if he was in his office last night or in bed. This morning, when he didn't come down for breakfast, I checked his office. Sometimes, he works here before going to the office. That's when I found him." Her voice cracked, and tears flowed again.

The neighbor brought cups of coffee along with cream and sugar. "I'll be in the kitchen if you need me," the woman said.

Aaron turned to Matt. "What about you? Did you hear

anything odd last night? Like a late visitor or a gunshot?"

He shook his head. Matt was a blonde, blue-eyed teen with muscles from playing sports. "I was at a friend's house, about two miles out of town. We went horseback riding, then I stayed the night. I didn't get home until a while ago after Mom called me about Dad."

Aaron found that interesting. No one was home when Cassie was here last night. Had she called ahead and planned it that way? Or had she just lucked out that he was alone?

"We're going to have a forensic team go over the scene today," Hughes said. "Is there somewhere else you can spend a night or two so you don't have to be here during that?"

"We can stay at a hotel," Jackie said.

Hughes nodded. "Thank you. We may have more questions later, so please keep in touch."

The forensic team arrived, and Hughes and Aaron watched them from the entryway as they dusted for prints, bagged the gun, and also bagged Tony's hand.

"They check for gunpowder residue," Aaron told Hughes when he saw the sheriff wrinkle his brow.

"Oh, yeah," Hughes said. "We rarely process crime scenes with bodies."

Aaron nodded. As a small-town sheriff's department, they processed crime scenes and car accidents but rarely had suicides or murders.

After a while, Hughes and Aaron decided to wait outside. It was difficult watching their late friend sitting in his chair with a hole in his head.

The coroner was still there, talking to Joe. Aaron approached him.

"Calvin. Do you have a time of death on Marty yet?"

Calvin turned to Aaron as Joe walked away. "It was in the report I sent over to the sheriff," he said.

"I haven't had a chance to read it. Do you remember?"

"From what I can tell, the mayor died between one and three that afternoon. There wasn't any food in his stomach, so I'm guessing he slept in late and missed breakfast," Calvin said.

"Could you tell if he'd been drinking?" Aaron asked.

"It's best to wait for the toxicology tests to come back," Calvin told him. "But I'm certain it wasn't a suicide. There were ligature marks around the lower part of his neck. Someone strangled him, then tossed him over the banister with a rope around his neck. His neck was broken, but that happened after he was already dead."

"Thanks, Calvin," Aaron said.

Hughes approached Aaron. "Drive me back to the station, then come back here and supervise this circus. Make sure Jackie and Matt leave for a hotel, and the paramedics take Tony to the morgue. I want an autopsy no matter what."

They got inside the car, and Aaron headed for the station. "What do you think you'll find with an autopsy that we don't already know?"

"I'm not sure," Hughes said. "I want to know if he was drinking or taking any drugs before he died. I want to make sure it was murder." He turned and stared at Aaron. "Shooting someone isn't as hard as lifting them over a balcony railing. She could have done this."

Aaron's hackles rose. "And Jackie could have done it too. Did you hear her? Tony and she were sleeping in separate bedrooms. Sounds like their marriage was on the skids. And what about Matt? It wouldn't be the first time a teenager killed his father."

"Jesus, Aaron! You're blaming the wife and kid? But you won't even consider that Cassie has the most obvious reason for killing Marty and Tony."

"I'm just saying there are more suspects than a woman planning her mother's funeral," Aaron said.

He pulled up at the back of the station, and Hughes moved to get out. "Just go back there and make sure everything's done right. And keep your suspicions to yourself. The last thing I need is the town thinking Jackie or Matt killed Tony."

Aaron watched as Hughes stepped out of the car and walked into the station. Then he pulled out of the lot and onto the street. Did he really believe that Tony's wife or kid could have killed him? No. But he didn't want to even consider that Cassie had done it.

His mind was racing by the time he'd returned to Tony's house. He'd seen Cassie at Marty's house around one-thirty in the afternoon on the day he died. And then again last night at Tony's house. Both men were dead, and Cassie had been at each house right before their deaths. Had she come home just to be with her dying mom and plan her funeral? Or did Cassie have a different plan in mind? A plan for revenge and murder.

CHAPTER SEVEN

It took three hours for the forensic team to finish their work and for Joe and his partner to transport Tony's body out of the house. Aaron had helped Jackie and Matt Wiles carry their luggage and pack it in their car. He made sure they had left before Tony's body was carried out.

The day had been exhausting. Craig had hung around the outside of the house with a panicked look in his eyes. He asked Aaron a thousand questions about Tony's death and paced a groove into the Wiles' perfectly manicured front lawn.

"Two of us are gone," he said in a ragged whisper so the other people at the scene wouldn't hear him. "Two! That only leaves Jason and me." He frowned at Aaron. "Maybe you too."

"Get ahold of yourself," Aaron told Craig. "You're the fire chief, for Christ's sake."

"Well, excuse me if I'm not used to having a target on my back," Craig said angrily. "What should I do? Should I leave town? Would she find me anyway? How are you going to protect me from her?"

Aaron sighed. "Go home, Craig. Call one of your buddies

from the fire department to have a few beers with you and calm down. *She* isn't behind this. Something else is going on."

"How can you be so sure?" Craig ran his hand through his short blond hair. "It can't be a coincidence that two of the men who hurt her are now dead."

"Those two men had jobs that caused enemies," Aaron reminded him. "Don't worry about it. Or leave town and take a vacation. Don't your parents live in Arizona? Go visit them."

"I can't leave right now," Craig said sullenly. "It's been dry all summer, and we're at the height of fire season. We're already short-staffed as it is."

Because you're a jerk of a boss, Aaron thought.

Craig studied him. "Why aren't you freaked out? You were the one who brought Cassie that night. You could be murdered, too."

"I was *tricked* into bringing Cassie there that night," Aaron said angrily. "And believe me, I've felt guilty about it all these years. I was happy to see she was still alive. And I wouldn't blame her if she did kill you four. But it's not her."

"How can you be so sure?" Craig insisted.

"Because I've known Cassie since we were toddlers. There isn't a mean bone in her body," Aaron said.

"That was then. This is now after she's had twenty years to seethe over what we did to her," Craig said.

"You and Jason are being stupid." Aaron was getting sick of them blaming the deaths on Cassie. "If you feel so guilty about what you did that night—and those other nights before that—then turn yourself in. Otherwise, shut up."

"I can see you're not going to be any help," Craig mumbled. He left in his nearing-forty-mid-life-crisis red sportscar.

"And you're a sitting duck driving around in that stupid

car," Aaron said quietly to himself.

After everyone had left, Aaron locked up the premises and put yellow tape over the door to warn people not to go inside. He glanced around and was surprised to see a security camera on a pole pointing toward the front door. *How had we missed that?* He circled the house and saw cameras on all four sides. As he got into his car, he called Jackie Wiles.

"Hi, Aaron. We're all checked into the hotel," she said.

"Great. I'm sure it will only be for a couple of days. And after we've finished going over the office, I can give you the number of a woman who cleans up, uh, sensitive areas like crime scenes."

"Okay," Jackie said. "Thanks."

"Say? I noticed you have security cameras around the house. Is there any chance I can look at the recent footage?" Aaron asked.

"Oh. Yeah. Those were Tony's idea. He was always paranoid because he put so many locals in jail. It's a simple app with a password. Just download the Blink app, and I'll give you the username and password."

"Oh, that's nice, but I can come by the hotel and just look at your phone," Aaron said. He was always surprised at how trusting people were of him just because he was a deputy.

"No sense in you taking the time to do that. This way, you can look over all the footage. There's a lot in the cloud. Maybe something will be helpful," Jackie said. She gave him the username and password and then said goodbye.

Aaron drove home to eat lunch before going back to work. He noticed that Cassie's car wasn't in the driveway and wondered where she was. Not that it mattered. It wasn't any of his business.

As he ate a plate of heated-up hotdish, Aaron downloaded the app on his phone. Then he signed in. Looking through the app, he found the recordings from the day before and watched them. Nothing strange occurred until he saw the one with Cassie arriving at Tony's front door. The timestamp was 8:10 p.m. The camera caught the side of Tony's surprised face standing in the doorway. Cassie said a few words, then Tony nodded, and she walked inside. At 8:30 p.m., Cassie was seen leaving the house. There was no sign of Tony standing in the doorway when she left.

Aaron sat back in his chair. If Hughes notices the cameras, he'll want to see the footage. These videos would bury Cassie. He looked at the two videos and saw he could download them and then delete them. So, he did. He'd have copies on his phone, but no one else would ever see the footage.

Watching the rest of the night's footage told Aaron nothing new. Matt never came and went, and Jackie came home around eleven, like she'd said. Since the cameras were motion-activated, nothing else set them off until the paramedics arrived the next day.

Why was Cassie at Tony's house for twenty minutes last night? And why did Tony let her in after being freaked out over Marty's death? He decided to keep the video to himself until he learned those answers.

* * *

The sheriff's department was in a frenzy when Aaron returned. People were camped out in front of the building, demanding answers. Two prominent men in town were dead. Why? News reporters from stations all around the state had vans parked on the street. It was mayhem.

Aaron drove around to the back of the building where civilians weren't allowed and parked his car. When he walked inside, the phones were still ringing off the hook, and everyone looked stressed.

"Where have you been?" Sheriff Hughes yelled at Aaron as he walked to his desk.

"I stayed at the house until everyone left and then had lunch," Aaron said. "What's going on here?"

"What does it look like?" Hughes shot back. "The whole town, no, the entire state, has gone berserk over the two murders."

"It hasn't been established yet whether Tony's was a suicide or murder," Aaron said.

"No, but Tony's wife has already talked to the press. She gave them all the information they wanted. She told them her husband was left-handed, but the gunshot was on the right side of his head." Hughes ran a hand over his short hair. "She was right on television saying all that. What's wrong with her? She wasn't even crying. She must have really hated Tony."

"She did say they were having problems," Aaron said.

"Yeah, but did she have to make it all public? We haven't even released information about Marty's death yet, and now she's put doubt in people's minds. Everyone believes we've had two murders," Hughes said.

Aaron studied Hughes a moment. The guy was agitated and his skin had turned red with anger. It looked like he was going to have a heart attack. "Let's go in your office so you can calm down," he suggested. "At this rate, it will be three deaths."

Hughes glared at him. "Maybe that's what she wants!"

"Come on." Aaron headed toward Hughes' office, and

thankfully, Hughes followed him. Everyone in the department stared at them, probably wondering who 'she' was.

Hughes sat at his desk, pulled out a bottle of whiskey and a glass from his bottom drawer, and poured himself a large portion.

"Great. That's going to help," Aaron said.

"Shut up." Hughes downed it in one gulp and poured more into the glass.

"When did you last eat?" Aaron asked. "You probably shouldn't be drinking that on an empty stomach."

"Oh, so now you're worried about me?" Hughes said. "I thought you were looking forward to me being the next one killed."

"Oh, for Pete's sake, Jason," Aaron said, disgusted. "Get over yourself. Let's sneak out of here and go to the diner up the road where those media people won't think to look for you. You need to eat."

Hughes agreed and put the bottle away in his desk.

Aaron drove his service car and headed north on the road out of town. About two miles up the road was a small diner that mostly truckers and locals used. The diner wasn't much to look at, but it had some of the best food in town.

They went inside and walked to a booth on the right-hand side. The booths ran along the big windows and the counter with stools was in the middle of the restaurant. A few truckers were sitting in booths and at the counter, but none of them seemed to care that two officers had come in.

"Hey, boys." Carin, the owner's wife, came up and automatically poured them each a cup of coffee. She was in her fifties with red-brown hair pulled up high on her head and wore too much make-up. But she was friendly, and everyone in town liked her. "What can I get you?"

"I'll have a cheeseburger and fries," Hughes said, not bothering to look up.

"And you, hon?" she asked Aaron.

"How about a piece of apple pie heated up," Aaron said, smiling.

She smiled back. "I'll be back in a jiff."

Hughes stared out the window, but he couldn't sit still. He was rubbing his hands together, fiddling with his coffee cup, and moving in his seat.

"What's going on with you?" Aaron asked. "You're usually so sure of yourself."

Hughes glared at him. "It's hard to be sure of anything when you have two dead bodies in the morgue."

"Yeah. It's been a tough week. But crap happens, and you have to pull yourself together," Aaron told him, then sipped his coffee. "Mm. Now, this is real coffee. This stuff can wake the dead."

"Not funny," Hughes said sharply. "On top of everything else, I got a call from Marty's wife last night. She said since they'd been separated for some time, she didn't see any reason to come home and plan his funeral. Can you believe that? She said to just cremate him and bury him in the spot he's already paid for beside his parents. How cold is that?"

"Wow. That's terrible," Aaron said, genuinely surprised. "I always liked her. But I know they had a lot of issues for years, plus they never had children. I guess she doesn't care about him. It's sad."

"The worst part is he was the mayor for the past four years. I can't just toss him in the ground. He'll need to have a memorial service. Otherwise, people will think we're covering up something. So now I have to plan a funeral." Hughes shook his head. "I hadn't planned on having to bury any of my friends so soon."

Aaron stared at Hughes a moment, holding back snide comments that came to him. He wanted to tell Jason that maybe they all deserved what was happening, but he thought better of it. "That's rough," was all he said.

Carin brought their food and warmed up their coffee. "Anything else, boys?"

"Can you turn back time, Carin?" Hughes asked.

Carin chuckled. "Wish I could. You guys have a heck of a mess on your hands, but you'll figure it all out." She left them to do just that.

Hughes took a few bites of his food and sipped his coffee. "You were right. I needed to eat. This might get me out of my funk," he said.

Aaron laughed. "I do like being right."

When Carin checked on them, Hughes asked for a glass of water, and she brought it with the check. "No hurry, boys. Just making sure I don't forget," she said.

The lunch crowd was thinning out as Hughes finished off his burger and fries. He sat back in the booth and looked more relaxed than when he'd come in.

"I guess we'll have to head back to the insanity," he said, sighing. "Maybe Calvin will have news on Tony, and I can give the press some information."

Aaron nodded. He'd finished his pie and was drinking the last of his coffee. "Tomorrow is Cassie's mother's funeral. It's at ten o'clock at the Lutheran Church on First Street. I feel like I should go, but I know I'm not welcome."

"Go," Hughes said, returning to his bossy self. "Keep an

eye on Cassie. At least she can't kill anyone while she's at the funeral."

Aaron shook his head. He was about to answer when the trucker behind him stood up and left, and Hughes' face lost all color.

"What?" Aaron asked. "What's wrong?"

"She's here," Hughes whispered, his voice shaking. "Cassie is here, and she's sitting there, glaring at me."

Aaron turned to look.

"Don't! Don't turn around, or she'll know we're talking about her," Hughes said. "How did we not see her when we came in?"

"Maybe she came in after we did," Aaron said.

Hughes shook his head. "No. I was looking out the window. She never got out of a car. Jeez! It's like she can appear out of nowhere."

"Get a grip, will you?" Aaron said, disgusted. "Cassie is just having lunch like we are."

"She's staring at me! I swear, it's like she's trying to kill me with her eyes," Hughes said. "We have to get out of here." He slid out of the booth and strode toward the door.

Aaron threw money on the table and waved to Carin. When he turned, he saw Cassie sitting in the last booth on the other end of the diner. She glanced up and saw him, then looked down again.

She doesn't look terrifying to me, Aaron thought.

He walked out to the car and slid inside. "I can't believe you're so afraid of Cassie," he said to Hughes.

"Let's just go!" Hughes said.

Aaron put the car in reverse and looked up to check his mirrors. When he did, he saw Cassie walking down the aisle inside the diner toward the table they'd just abandoned. She stopped, reached for something, then turned to leave.

What in the heck was she taking?

Glancing at Hughes, he realized he hadn't been watching the diner. His head was down, looking at his phone. Aaron figured he'd just keep what he saw to himself.

As he drove back to the station, Aaron thought about Cassie. He didn't believe she'd murdered anyone, especially men who could easily overpower her. But what was she up to? He had no idea.

CHAPTER EIGHT

One more day until her mother's funeral, and then Cassie had to concentrate on selling the house. She sat at the kitchen table and sighed. She'd been carefully packing up her mother's wedding china. This was hard. She'd known her mother was getting older, but she'd expected she'd be alive for a few more years. Cassie had hoped to talk her mother into moving out to California so she'd be closer, and they could see each other more. But that never happened, and now, here she was, wrapping newspaper around delicate plates and cups to ship home.

Cassie had the television on as she worked all morning and was surprised when a news bulletin came on the local news. "District Attorney Found Dead," the headline said. Cassie turned the sound up and was surprised to see Tony's wife speaking with a news reporter in front of a local hotel.

Cassie watched with interest. The wife said it was a gunshot wound to the head but that Tony had been shot from right to left. It couldn't be suicide because Tony was left-handed. Tony's wife showed no emotion while she spoke. Either she was in shock, or she didn't care that her husband was dead.

Cassie clicked off the television and stared out the window. It was a little after noon, and she watched as Aaron's service car pulled into his driveway. She figured he was home for lunch. Aaron seemed very domestic, cooking his own meals and always coming home for lunch. He would have made someone a good husband. She wondered why he'd never married. The other guys, except for Jason, had been married, but none of the women had stayed around. Well, except for Tony's wife, but by the look of it, their marriage must have been on the outs, or else she would have seemed a bit more upset that someone shot him.

After finishing packing the china, Cassie decided to get a bite to eat. She was tired of making lunchmeat sandwiches at home, and Mrs. Orton's hot dish was growing stale in the refrigerator. Fresh food would taste good.

Not wanting to see anyone in town, Cassie decided to drive out to the diner on the highway. Locals ate there, but mainly truckers and travelers did, so she didn't think she'd run into anyone she knew.

When she arrived at the diner, she was disappointed to see a sheriff's car parked out front. Not wanting to be seen, she parked on the side of the building and made her way to the front door. Off to the right, sitting in a booth, were Aaron and Jason. Ugh! When she entered the diner, she took a quick left and made her way to the back booth. With all the bodies between them, she hoped they wouldn't see her.

"Afternoon, hon," the waitress said with a smile on her painted lips. "Would you like some coffee?"

Cassie smiled back. She didn't know this woman, and she liked it that way. "No, thank you. But I'd love a Diet Coke, please. And do you have a Chef's Salad on the menu?"

"You bet we do," the waitress, whose name tag read Carin, said. "I'll be right back with your drink." She turned and walked away.

Cassie took out her phone to text James. She missed her husband and was eager to go home. But she hadn't asked him to take off of work to come here because it would have been weird having him in her hometown. As far as she was concerned, this place was a nightmare that she wanted to see in her rear-view mirror.

"Here you go, sweetie," Carin said, placing her drink on the Formica tabletop. "The salad will be here in a minute."

Cassie watched her leave. Twenty years ago, when this diner was new, the owners had been a young couple looking to make it rich. Apparently, their dreams hadn't come true because Cassie didn't recognize the waitress or the cook who she could see working in the kitchen through the pass-through. At least some things changed in this small town.

"Here you go, hon," Carin said, setting down a nice, fresh salad. "And don't feel rushed; I'm just leaving the check so I don't forget to give it to you." She chuckled and tapped her pencil to her head. "This old brain forgets a lot these days."

Cassie laughed. "That's because you're so busy. I'd forget things too if I was running around as much as you."

Carin smiled and went down the row of tables, refilling coffee cups.

Before eating, Cassie glanced around the bodies and heads in front of her and saw that Aaron and Jason were still there, deep in conversation. She supposed with two murders or suicides on their hands, they were crazy busy. She just hoped they were too busy with their thoughts to notice her here.

Cassie thought about all she had to do before leaving town.

She'd packed up a lot of the house so far, but there was still so much left. She'd talked to the real estate woman about selling it with the furniture, and the woman had thought that might be a good idea. The new owners could keep it or sell it for a little extra money. It was just the personal belongings that Cassie had to either keep, sell, or give away. And that was a big job. Her mother had kept nearly everything they'd ever owned, along with all of Cassie's childhood toys and teenage belongings. There was so much to wade through that it was overwhelming.

And then there were the two other things she had to do—things that she wasn't looking forward to. But it had to be done because it was something she had to know for sure.

Cassie finished her salad as the place cleared out. With everyone out of the booths, she had a clear view of the back of Aaron's head and Jason's fat face. As she looked down the row of booths, Jason looked up and turned pale. For an instant, she almost looked away, but then, upon seeing his reaction, she just kept staring at him. *Let him freak out,* she thought. Two of his best friends were dead under mysterious circumstances. Obviously, Jason was thinking he'd be next.

Aaron turned around, saw Cassie and smiled, then turned back. Cassie kept staring. Suddenly, Jason scrambled out of the booth and practically ran out the door. Cassie wanted to laugh out loud but held it in. She looked down at her phone for a moment when it pinged that James had answered her. When she looked up, Aaron was gone too.

Glancing out the window, Cassie saw the two men in the sheriff's cruiser. She glanced again at their empty table. Carin was busy cleaning the counter. Cassie had an idea. She dropped money on the table for her lunch and a big tip, then walked to the table Aaron and Jason had just abandoned. Making sure Carin was preoccupied, Cassie lifted Jason's glass of water, poured what was left in it into his coffee cup, and slipped the empty glass into her purse. She turned and headed for the door, calling out a goodbye to Carin as she went.

One more item checked off her list of things to do.

CHAPTER NINE

The next morning, Aaron decided to go to Mrs. Sanders' funeral even if Cassie wouldn't want him there. They'd been neighbors all his life, and he thought it might look odd if he didn't attend. So, instead of putting on his uniform, he dressed in a nice pair of slacks, a dress shirt, and a tie. He could come home and change afterward.

Yesterday afternoon had been hectic. Hughes was a jittery mess when they returned to the station, and he poured himself a few more drinks. They received a preliminary report on Tony's death later that afternoon, which didn't help matters. While there was no question as to Tony's death being the result of a gunshot wound, the forensic team found some interesting information. No gunshot residue was found on either of Tony's hands. There was no way Tony could have pulled the trigger himself.

Hughes freaked out from that information. What was also strange was there had been no evidence of a fight. Tony had been sitting calmly at his desk when he was shot. Clearly, the person who shot him knew him well, or Tony was comfortable enough with them to not worry when they drew close enough to shoot him.

Sheriff Hughes decided to wait another day to have a press conference. He wanted to speak to Tony's wife and son once more and check out their alibis before he made any decisions about the case.

As Aaron drove to the funeral, he thought about yesterday's findings. Cassie had been at Tony's house during the coroner's estimated time of death. But would Tony have been comfortable enough with Cassie in his office to not notice her pointing a gun at him? And what were they doing in his office? The idea of blackmail went through Aaron's mind, but then he dismissed it. He had trouble believing after all these years, Cassie would go to each guy who'd attacked her and blackmail them. But what other reason would make her go see them?

Aaron arrived at the church and parked on the street. The place was packed. Mrs. Sanders had lived in town for decades and had touched many people. Christine Sanders had been a nurse before she had Cassie, and when Cassie was old enough to attend school, Mrs. Sanders started working as the school nurse in the elementary school. It was the perfect job for her so she could have her summers off with her daughter. So nearly everyone in town knew Mrs. Sanders from the school.

Aaron waited for the time the service was to begin, then went inside. Everyone was already seated, so he slipped into a back pew. He planned on leaving the church before Cassie saw him after the service.

Cassie and a few of her cousins who lived in the area were the only family there. The principal of the grade school stood and spoke about how beloved Mrs. Sanders was to the children of the community. There were prayers and songs, and just as the service came to an end, Aaron slipped out.

On the drive home to change, Aaron thought how sad it was that Cassie had so little family to help her grieve. The whole community was behind her, but family was important. Aaron had only a few relatives left also. His sister and her family and his mother, who now lived with her new husband in South Carolina, were his only relatives. He'd never married, which he regretted, nor had children. Every relationship Aaron ever had ended abruptly, with the woman going off to eventually marry someone else. He'd dated many wonderful women, but he never felt he was worthy of marrying them. After what had happened to Cassie, because of him, he worried he'd hurt someone else. Now, he was basically alone.

"Where were you?" Sheriff Hughes asked Aaron as he walked into the station. "It's late."

"I was at Mrs. Sanders' funeral, remember?" Aaron said.

"Oh." Hughes looked uncomfortable. "So, how was it?"

"Sad," Aaron said. "But half the town was there, or so it seemed. It was a nice funeral."

"Oh," Hughes said again. "Good. She was a nice lady."

"Yes, she was," Aaron said. "What's going on here?"

"You and I are going to speak with Jackie and Matt at one o'clock this afternoon," Hughes said. "I want to make sure there aren't any holes in their stories. I checked their alibies, and they were gone that evening, but Jackie admitted to being home at eleven o'clock. The timeline was from eight to midnight, which doesn't narrow it down very well, so Jackie could still be a suspect."

"Do you think Jackie Wiles is the type of woman who could kill her husband and then happily go off and sleep soundly?" Aaron asked.

"I don't know. I spent time with Tony, but rarely at their house except for a meal or two over the years. Maybe she was that angry with him. Everyone knows he was sleeping with every young woman in town who'd have him."

"Maybe one of the other women shot him," Aaron said. "He could have made promises he didn't keep."

"Maybe," Hughes replied. "But that's a long list of suspects. Let's start with the family. Matt was staying at a friend's house outside of town. They rode horses and then played video games until midnight, the kid's mother said, and then all was quiet. Matt could have slipped out, driven home, shot his dad, and gone back."

"Isn't he a straight-A student and lead player for the basketball team?" Aaron asked.

Hughes shrugged. "That doesn't make him a saint."

Aaron thought for a moment, then decided to mention what he knew. "I learned that Tony had cameras outside the house. We can go through the footage and see if anyone shows up on it."

"Really? I didn't notice that," Hughes said. "Good. See if you can access it and look through them."

"I will," Aaron told him. He'd wait a while before telling Hughes that no one had entered or left the house. At least, no one Aaron was willing to share with him.

After speaking with Jackie and Matt, neither Aaron nor Sheriff Hughes felt they were suspects. Jackie admitted to being separated from Tony and would eventually divorce him, but they hadn't wanted to do that until Matt was in college. She said she knew Tony had had several affairs, but she didn't care anymore. She'd been looking forward to getting her half of the money and leaving.

Matt, on the other hand, was devastated by his father's death. They were close, and neither Hughes nor Aaron could see any animosity in him toward his father.

"Cripes. The last thing I want to do is talk to every bar waitress in town and ask about their affair with Tony," Hughes said after they'd spoken to the family. "I'd rather just call it a suicide and move on."

"We can't do that," Aaron said sternly. "We're supposed to find the truth."

"Do you want to find the truth and hurt Tony's family in the process?" Hughes asked. "And what if the truth is that Cassie did it? Would you like that?"

Aaron shook his head. "She didn't do it. I was able to look through the footage on the cameras that night, and she doesn't appear in any of them. Jackie came home at eleven like she said, and that was it. No movement until the next morning."

Hughes eyed him. "How convenient."

That evening, Sheriff Hughes had another press conference at five, just in time for the evening news, saying that both deaths were still under investigation. He alluded to the fact that they could have been suicides, but they were still looking into them.

Aaron stood behind him, wanting to shake his head. Someone killed both men, he was certain. But who?

* * *

After the news conference, Aaron headed home. As he drove into his driveway, he was surprised to see Cassie sitting alone on her home's front stoop. Aaron stepped out of his car and waved to her, and surprisingly, she waved back. Encouraged by her actions, he slowly made his way to the front of her house.

"Why didn't you stay for the reception after the funeral?" Cassie asked, looking straight at him.

"Oh. You knew I was there?" Aaron was embarrassed. "Sorry. I slipped in and out because I figured you wouldn't want to see me there."

She shrugged. "I don't know if I care one way or the other. It's been a hard day."

"I'm sorry," he said again. "I wanted to go for your mother. I just didn't want to cause you any more distress."

Cassie laughed. "These last two weeks have been nothing but distressing." She looked up at him again, then slid over on the steps to give him space to sit down.

Aaron hesitated, then gingerly sat next to her. "Can I do anything to help?"

She shook her head. "No. But it's nice of you to offer, considering we're not friends anymore."

"I wish we still were," he said. "But I get it. There aren't enough apologies in the world to make up for what happened to you," Aaron said.

Cassie looked down at her forearm, where she had a long burn scar. "And even if I don't think about it, this scar reminds me."

Aaron sighed. "At least you survived it," he said. "That's something."

She frowned at him. "Those first few years, I wished I hadn't. I had nightmares constantly. I had trouble concentrating on my schoolwork and nearly flunked out of college. I didn't make friends easily because I trusted no one. If I hadn't been living with my aunt, who's a therapist, I don't think I would have made it through."

"I'm sorry," Aaron said again. And he meant it. He wished he could change everything, but he couldn't.

"My parents knew, you know." She glanced over at him. "They knew who attacked me and nearly killed me."

Aaron looked into her lovely blue eyes. Her looks hadn't changed, but her demeanor had. She was harder. Tougher. "You told them?"

"Yes. I told the police at the hospital that it was strangers who took me from the parking lot at the graduation party and attacked me. But when we got home, I told my parents the truth. It took all the strength I had left to stop my dad from taking his baseball bat to your house and beating you to death. He wanted to beat you all to death."

Aaron dropped his head. "Maybe he should have. We all deserved it. Still do."

"That wouldn't have solved anything, though. Like you said that night, each of those kids, except you, had fathers who could sweep everything under the rug. They would have ruined my dad and mom's careers and lives. Letting it go was the best thing to do." Cassie looked up at the darkening sky. "I kept hoping karma would get you all. I guess it finally is."

Aaron watched her for a moment. "Someone shot Tony. I know that because they shot him on the right side of his head, and he was left-handed."

She tilted her head and gazed at him. "Do you think I did it?"

"No. But I think you would have liked to have done it. And I think you should have."

She lifted her brows. "Wow. I guess you weren't his friend."

"I haven't been friends with any of them since that night," Aaron said. "The only reason I work with Jason is because his father hired me first, and then Jason was finally hired. Otherwise, I would never see him."

"Why'd you come back here to live? You could have been a deputy anywhere in the country," Cassie said.

"I don't know. It's familiar, I guess. And they had an opening when I graduated. Maybe I was afraid to go anywhere else. Or maybe it was just easy."

"Hm. I lived with my aunt in California all through college and until I married. She helped me through the trauma of what happened, and I became a trauma nurse and work in the emergency department at a hospital. There's nothing easy about that. I guess I wanted to help others like me," Cassie said. "And you know what? Every time a rape victim comes into the ER and I look into her eyes, I see myself all over again. Trauma like that never leaves you. It becomes a part of you."

"I'm sorry," Aaron said again. "I'd always hoped you'd gone away and moved on with your life, leaving this nightmare behind. I never thought of it becoming a part of you. How stupid am I?"

She smiled for the first time since she'd returned. "Do you really want me to answer that?"

He grinned. "Probably not. So, now that the funeral is over, how much longer are you staying?"

Cassie sighed. "I have the real estate woman coming tomorrow to put this place on the market. I think I'll sell most of the furniture with it, but there's still a lot of personal stuff to pack and go through. Once I get those things packed up, I can leave."

"If you need any help," he started to say, but she interrupted him.

"No, thank you, Aaron. I'm glad we had a chance to talk

civilly, but I can't see myself spending any amount of time with you. Especially going through old boxes from my childhood."

His heart dropped. He'd hoped this conversation would have brought them closer. "Okay. I get it. But if there's anything else you need, just holler." He stood to leave, then turned back to her. "Cass?"

She smiled wanly. "I know. You're sorry. I accept that, but I can't absolve you of your guilt for what happened. I don't have enough forgiveness in me for that."

He nodded, then headed to his own house.

CHAPTER TEN

Cassie went inside her mother's house as the sun set. She headed to the kitchen and pulled out a bottle of wine from the refrigerator. She'd stopped at the liquor store after the funeral and reception and bought a bottle of chardonnay on impulse. Now, after her long day and after having talked with Aaron, she definitely needed a glass to relax.

Today had been a long, tiresome day. Planning the funeral had been hard, but sitting through the service and having to speak with each person who'd attended had been excruciating. Cassie had been shocked by how many people had attended the service. It was nice that they wanted to say goodbye to her mother, but it had been difficult for Cassie. Each person was curious why they hadn't seen Cassie in years and blatantly asked her personal questions that she didn't feel comfortable answering. She knew they'd all meant well, but it had drained her completely.

As she sipped the wine, Cassie's phone rang. She answered right away, thankful it was her husband.

"How was the funeral today?" he asked gently.

Cassie sighed. She missed her home so much and wished James was sitting with her right now. "It went well. There was a big turnout, and people had a lot of nice things to say."

"That's good," he said. "Did anyone pry?"

He knew her so well. "Yes, but I gave vague answers and turned to the next person. I think a lot of people thought I didn't get along with my mother, and that's why I never came home. But the people closest to my parents knew that they visited me often and we had a good relationship. Still, it was a trying day."

"I'm sorry," he said gently. "I wish you'd let me come there and help. You still have the house to pack up, and that's a big job."

"I know. But honestly, I don't want this town and my bad memories of the last night I lived here to taint your life. Once the house is packed up, I'm gone for good."

"Okay. I'll do things your way. But if you need me, I can be there on the next plane," James said, sounding concerned.

Cassie took a sip of wine, then said, "Aaron came to Mom's funeral. And I talked to him this evening. I'm trying to process my feelings about him." James knew Cassie's story, so he knew how much strength it had taken Cassie just to talk to Aaron.

"Do you feel safe there?" he asked. "Would any of them ever hurt you again?"

"I'm fine," she said. "Aaron would never hurt me on purpose, and I'm not getting close enough to him for anything to happen. And I'm keeping my distance from the worst one of all, Jason."

"That's smart. Just finish what you need to do and get out of that town," James said.

"It's all almost over. And I can move forward and truly put

this place behind me for good."

After hanging up, Cassie wondered why she hadn't told James that two of the men were already dead. Frankly, she was relieved they were dead, but she didn't think James would understand. He was a doctor who saved lives. He wouldn't understand why their deaths would set her free. *Just finish what you need to do and get out of that town,* James had said. Cassie was determined to do just that.

* * *

Aaron was supposed to have the next day off but instead was talked into making the funeral arrangements for Marty. Jason said he didn't have time and really didn't know what needed to be done. Since Aaron had helped his mother with his father's arrangements, he agreed to do it. But he understood it was just another way of Jason using him even though they weren't friends.

Aaron went to the morgue first to ask when they'd release the body and learned the mortuary could have it any time. So, he went to Smith Brothers Mortuary and talked to them about cremation and having a service in their chapel. He arranged for Marty to be cremated, per Marty's wife's instructions, and set a date for the funeral. After that, he arranged to have the cemetery prepare the plot for burial next to Marty's parents which Marty already owned. It was a lot to take care of, and Aaron resented having to do this on his day off for someone he was no longer friends with.

He stopped at the sheriff's station after he'd finished making arrangements to see if there was any new information about Tony's case. Sheriff Hughes had just returned from lunch and waved him into the office.

"Did you get everything settled for Marty?" he asked.

"Most of it," Aaron said. "I called his wife and told her she had to find someone to write up the obituary and decide what to put on the headstone. She acted annoyed, but she agreed. Sheesh!" Aaron ran his hand through his brown hair. "What did Marty do to her to make her hate him so much? They were married for twelve years. You'd think she'd care that he's dead."

Hughes shook his head. "Marty never talked about his wife, other than the usual ball and chain type of comments or that she spent too much money. I've never been married, so I don't know what goes on in a marriage."

Aaron studied Hughes for a moment. "Don't you find it odd that everyone from our high school group is either not married or their marriages failed?"

"That includes you, too," Hughes said gruffly.

"Yeah. I know. Why didn't you ever get married?"

"Who knows? Most women are clingy and want too much. I like being free."

"Yeah, right." Aaron knew that Jason was always too rough with the women he dated. None of them wanted to stay around to see if he'd get rougher.

"Why haven't you ever married?" Hughes asked.

Aaron sighed. "I guess I thought I didn't deserve to be happy. Not after what happened to Cassie."

Hughes snorted. "You're such a wimp, you know that?"

Aaron narrowed his eyes at Hughes. "You know, Cassie told me her father and mother knew all along who had hurt her. She told the police at the hospital a different story, but she told her father the truth. He wanted to kill all of us. Too bad Cassie stopped him."

Hughes sat up at his desk, looking startled. "They knew? This whole time?"

"Yes."

"Well, I'm glad they never did anything about it," Hughes said.

Aaron shook his head. Jason was never going to be sorry for what he did as a teenager. For all Aaron knew, Jason was still raping and killing women. He wouldn't put it past him.

"What's going on with Tony's case?" Aaron asked, sounding all business again.

"Not much. They're going to check for fingerprints on the gun and on the desk surface, but they don't know who to compare them to. Other than Tony and the family, we have no clue who could have killed him. This might end up as a cold case."

"Wouldn't surprise me," Aaron said as he stood. "See you tomorrow."

Aaron left and headed for the pub downtown. He was hungry and could use a beer.

"Hey, Aaron. You off today?" the waitress, Andi Stratten, asked him as she brought him a menu.

Aaron had chosen to sit in the back corner where it was dark and quiet. "Yeah. It's been a long week. I'll have a cheeseburger, fries, and beer on tap."

"Okay." She smiled at him. Andi was in her mid-twenties and had long blond hair and bright blue eyes. She was definitely a good-looking woman. "I heard about Tony. How terrible! He was a regular here."

Aaron nodded. *I'll bet he was,* he thought. "Yeah. It was terrible. We're still working on finding the person who killed him."

"I hope you do. It's scary, thinking someone is running around killing people in this small town." Andi smiled again. "I'll go get your order in and grab that beer." She sauntered off, her hips moving seductively.

Aaron thought Andi didn't appear that torn up about Tony's death. He knew that many of the young waitresses in town had cozied up to Tony at one time or another. That's why Aaron stayed far away from most of them despite their being attractive.

Craig walked in wearing his uniform. He glanced around, adjusting his eyes to the dark, saw Aaron, and headed for his table. "Hey, Aaron. Mind if I sit?"

Do I have a choice? Aaron thought. "Sure. What's going on?"

Craig shifted nervously in his seat. "I just had a weird conversation. I need a beer." He waved Andi over.

"Aren't you on duty?" Aaron asked.

"Don't be so picky. I've had a hard couple of days," Craig said sharply. When Andi brought Aaron's beer, Craig ordered one too.

"What's the word on Tony's death?" Craig asked after Andi walked away.

"Nothing, yet. It takes time going through the evidence," Aaron told him.

"What evidence?"

"Fingerprints. Timelines. We really don't have much to go on."

Andi brought Craig's beer, and he took a long swig. "Aren't you freaking out? I mean, first Marty and then Tony. Who's next? It could be you, me, or Jason."

Aaron laughed. "You need to calm down. Marty and Tony

had jobs that attracted enemies. I doubt if you do. You save houses, businesses, and lives."

Craig glanced around, then spoke quietly. "People don't like me. I know my crew can't stand me, and I've made a few enemies in town. And then there's Cassie."

"Leave Cassie out of this," Aaron said sharply. "She hasn't hurt anyone."

Craig took another long drink. "Would you blame her if she did want to kill us? I wouldn't. I can't believe I went along with that crap back then. Stupid Jason. He always thought he was so cool. He's a creep; that's what he is."

"Really?" Aaron was surprised by his words. "Then why are you friends?"

"Do I have a choice? He's the sheriff. I'm the fire chief. We have to get along. But I wish I hadn't been his friend in high school. I was an idiot."

"Yeah. That makes two of us," Aaron said.

Andi brought his food, and Aaron took a few bites while Craig downed his beer.

"I'd better go. I just needed to calm down for a bit," Craig said.

"Who upset you?" Aaron asked.

"I'd rather not say. Our conversation just unnerved me. See you later." Craig pushed back his chair, tossed money on the table for the beer, and left.

Aaron watched him leave and wondered who he'd talked to that made him so jittery.

"He's one big ball of creepiness," Andi said when she came to check if Aaron wanted another beer.

"Why do you say that?" Aaron asked.

"I'm sorry if he's your friend, but I can't stand Craig

Becker. The way he treats women when he's drunk is horrible. He makes my skin crawl."

"Interesting," Aaron said. "And he's not my friend, so don't worry about it."

Aaron placed a hefty tip on the table when he left. Andi was always sweet, but he was happy she'd confided in him about Craig. As far as Aaron was concerned, Craig was a creep.

The rest of the day and evening, Aaron stayed home. He did his laundry and some work around the house and even mowed the lawn. As he worked, he noticed Cassie walking from one room to another in her mother's house and figured she was going through everything. He knew what a big job that was because he'd helped his mother sort through things before she remarried and moved.

As Aaron grilled a steak for dinner, he thought back to something Cassie had said yesterday. *"Like you said that night."* That night. That terrible night twenty years ago that changed everyone's life, especially Cassie's. He remembered it as clearly as if it happened yesterday.

The sound of car engines starting and tires on the dirt road made Aaron open his eyes. The guys were leaving. Aaron looked up and frowned. He saw flames through the cabin's small back window. He jumped out of his truck and smelled gasoline and smoke. Christ! They'd set the cabin on fire.

And Cassie was in there.

Aaron took off in a sprint toward the cabin.

He felt the heat coming off the building long before he made it to the window. Careful not to touch anything, he looked inside. Cassie was curled up like a ball on the rug. Was she dead? Suddenly, her arm moved. Cassie was alive. He had to get her out of there.

He studied the room through the window. The flames weren't at the door yet and, surprisingly, hadn't touched the rug. Once they did, it would go up immediately. If he hurried, he could get her out.

Aaron ran around to the door. He knew the handle was hot, so he wrapped his shirt tail around his hand and quickly opened the door. Flames leapt out, and he jumped back. Opening the door caused the fire to spread quicker, so he had to be fast. Placing his arm over his nose and mouth, Aaron ran inside.

It took a moment for him to make out Cassie's form on the rug through the thick smoke. He ran to her, the flames already licking at her skin. Aaron lifted her up and ran out the door. He didn't stop running until he got to the truck. Laying Cassie on the passenger side of the seat, he tried to wake her up. "Cassie? Cassie? Are you okay?"

Cassie slowly moved and looked up at him with wild eyes. Her face was swollen and turning black and blue, and her arm was seriously burned. Despite the heat of the evening, she began to shake.

Aaron grabbed the blanket he kept inside his truck and covered her, but she suddenly sat up and screamed.

"It's okay. It's okay," he said soothingly. "I'm here. I got you out."

She stared at him again, but her eyes looked blank. Aaron saw her dress was in rags and nearly ripped off, and her torso and legs were terribly bruised. Anger rose inside him. He wished he had gone into the cabin and killed them all.

He readjusted the blanket around Cassie, so it was over her shoulders. Then he ran around to the driver's side and jumped in. "I'll take you to the hospital," he said. Then he rethought that. There would be questions at the local hospital, and Sheriff Hughes,

Jason's dad, or one of his deputies would be called in because of Cassie's condition. That would cause a multitude of problems for Cassie and her parents—not for the boys who did this.

He started the truck and drove to the highway, careful not to hit every bump. Cassie moaned with each movement, and tears trickled down her cheeks.

"I'll take you to the hospital in the next town," he said once he hit the highway. "You'll get better care there, and maybe they'll ask fewer questions."

Aaron drove as fast as he dared and kept glancing over at Cassie. She was sitting straight up now and staring out the front window. She looked like she was in shock.

"I'm sorry," Aaron said, as tears filled his eyes. He swiped them away. "I'm sorry I couldn't save you from them. I'm sorry I brought you there. Oh, Cassie," he stopped, unable to speak as he choked up.

Cassie turned and stared at him. Just stared. He realized that saying he was sorry wasn't going to change anything for her.

Finally, they made it to the hospital. Aaron drove his truck up to the emergency room door as close as he dared. He knew there were cameras outside the door and didn't dare have his truck on the video. It pained him that he thought about protecting himself and his family when he should have been worried about Cassie. But if he were caught with Cassie in this condition, he'd be blamed for it, and that would ruin his life and that of his parents. He couldn't do that to them.

"I can't go in with you," he said gently. "I'll ruin my family's life if I do. Jason, Tony, Craig, and Marty will never be blamed for what happened to you. Their parents are too influential for them to ever have to pay for this. And I can't afford to have my parents' lives ruined either."

Cassie just stared at him. He wasn't sure if she understood his words or not.

"Go on in. Let them help you," Aaron said gently. He felt guilty for what he'd just said to her. "Forget what I just said. Tell them the truth. We should all pay for what happened to you."

Cassie blinked, and a single tear ran down her cheek.

Aaron got out of the truck and ran around to open Cassie's door. He carefully helped her out and wrapped the blanket tightly around her. "I'm sorry," he said again, but he doubted Cassie heard him. She stumbled across the walkway and through the automatic sliding glass doors.

As Aaron drove away, he felt sick to his stomach. He'd never forgive himself for tonight. Never.

And Aaron never did. As he sat eating dinner, he thought about the teenage boy he'd been and the man he was now. Now, he would have killed those guys for even thinking about doing what they did to Cassie. Becoming an officer had given him the strength and courage to fight back. But back then, he'd been a coward, and he cringed every time he thought of leaving her there at the hospital in the middle of the night and driving away. No. He'd never forgive himself for as long as he lived.

Later that evening, Aaron made a bowl of popcorn and sat in front of his television, hoping to distract himself from his nightmare memories. As he scrolled through the movies on Netflix, he noticed car lights coming from Cassie's house. He stood and watched as Cassie's car pulled out of the driveway and headed down the street. Looking at his watch he saw it was six-forty-five.

"Where is she going?" he said aloud in the empty room. It wasn't any of his business, but he couldn't help but wonder.

CHAPTER ELEVEN

Cassie awoke with a dry mouth and severe headache the next day. Sitting up, she instantly regretted drinking the entire bottle of wine. After showering and brushing her teeth, she felt a little better. She ate some toast, and soon, she felt almost like her old self. Almost.

The real estate agent, Angie Crawford, arrived on time for their eleven o'clock appointment. She was a tall, slender blonde with a bubbly personality that caused Cassie's headache to return. Angie walked around the house, taking measurements and asking questions. Then she said she'd take photos after Cassie removed the boxes so it wouldn't look so cluttered. By twelve-thirty, Cassie was glad to see the back side of the perky Angie as she exited through the front door.

"At least she's eager and will sell the house," Cassie told herself.

Hungry for healthy food, Cassie drove to the local grocery store and stocked up on fresh vegetables, fruits, and whole-wheat bread. She filled her cart with food so she could eat at the house more often, then drove home with her groceries. As she made herself a sandwich for lunch, with Oreos on the side, Cassie thought about all the things she still needed to do around town. She still owed the florist the second payment for the casket flowers, and she needed to stop at the mortuary to pay them for their services. Luckily, her mother had a healthy savings account and a small life insurance policy that more than paid for the funeral expenses.

She decided to run her errands after lunch so all the bills were paid. Then she could concentrate on packing up the rest of the house.

And she still had one more little detail to take care of.

Cassie drove downtown and stopped first at Hadley Flowers and Gifts to pay off her account. Then she went to Smith Brothers' Mortuary and paid her bill there. She also picked up several packets of thank-you notes. Many of the attendees had left sympathy cards, and Cassie planned on going through them once the house was packed and she was back in California.

As Cassie walked to her car, she realized she was right next to the fire department. She stopped a moment and stared at the old brick building built in 1899. She knew Craig Becker was the fire chief now, so he would most likely be inside the building. Taking a deep breath, she decided to go inside and check off the last item on her list.

One of the two tall garage doors was open, so Cassie walked inside. The building didn't seem so large on the outside, but inside was cavernous. One young man wearing jeans and a tight t-shirt was standing on a ladder truck, polishing the chrome. He looked down at her and smiled.

"Can I help you?" he called out to her. His voice echoed in the large garage.

"I'm looking for the fire chief," she called back.

He pointed to a set of glass doors. "Go through there and to your left. His office is right there."

"Thanks," Cassie said. She went through the glass doors which led into the office building. Taking a left, she saw an open office door at the end. As she approached, Craig came out, talking to one of his crew. When he finally looked up, he went pale.

Cassie stared at him for a moment, then approached him. With each step she took toward Craig, she saw his face growing whiter. *Good, you should be scared,* she thought, relishing the moment.

She stopped in front of him. "We need to talk."

The other man smiled at her and walked away while Craig continued to stare. Finally, he found his voice. "Why are you here?"

"I just need a moment of your time. That's all," Cassie said sternly. "It's the least you can do after what you and your friends did to me."

Craig was visibly shaking. "Are you going to kill me, too?" he asked in a hushed voice.

Cassie laughed. "No. I didn't kill your friends, and I don't plan on killing you. I just need five minutes."

Craig frowned. He looked confused. Glancing around the office, he finally said. "Can we meet after work? I'd prefer not to talk here in the office. I'm done at seven."

Cassie sighed. "Fine. I'll drop by your house after seven. And don't do anything stupid, okay? I just need one thing from you, and that's it."

Craig nodded. The color still hadn't returned to his face.

Cassie turned and left the building. She was not a mean-spirited person, and she hated confrontation, but she did feel a little satisfaction at making Craig nervous.

Returning home, Cassie began packing more boxes of the things she wanted to keep. It was a hard job, deciding which part of her childhood to keep and which part to sell or toss. As she packed boxes, she thought about the men who'd nearly killed her and almost destroyed her life. Two were dead, and two were left. Even though they had all continued their lives like normal people, going to school, getting good jobs, some even marrying and having kids, she wondered if deep down they were still the horrible teenagers who'd hurt her.

She also thought about everything her parents went through after the attack. Her father wasn't the happy-go-lucky person he'd been before it happened and grew cynical about people with age. Her mother, who had adored working with younger kids, grew wary of the children around her at school. She'd watch for signs of bullying in the kids to ensure another Jason, Craig, Marty, and Tony wouldn't exist. Cassie also knew her parents hated that they couldn't see her more often. But neither could they uproot their lives and leave their jobs that they'd spent years at. Not only had her attack changed her, but it had changed them, too. And Cassie had always felt guilty about that.

Now, two of the offenders were dead, and she couldn't care less. Cassie knew that was awful, but it was true. Did that make her a terrible person? Maybe. But after she was done with this town, she hoped she wouldn't bring her anger back home with her. Anger ate you up inside and turned you sour toward life. She didn't want that.

But she was still glad they were dead.

That evening, Cassie made a salad for herself and ate some crackers with it. She watched the evening news on her mother's old television and puttered around the house until six forty-five. Then she got in her car and headed to Craig's house. He was the last one on her list, and then she'd be almost ready to leave town.

Finally.

CHAPTER TWELVE

Aaron arrived at the sheriff's station at nine o'clock sharp the next morning. He was happy to see the press had given up and no one was outside blocking the entrance. He waved to Rhonda and headed for his desk. Duds was sitting at his desk, staring at his computer.

"Hey, Dudley. What's up?" Aaron asked cheerfully. Duds was usually in a good mood, but this morning, he looked unhappy.

"I had to come in early this morning and couldn't go fishing," he said. "I don't even understand why. Nothing new is going on."

"Hm." Aaron looked around. "Is the Sheriff in?"

"He's chewing out Frank in his office. Apparently, Frank decided to pull a Columbo and started interrogating every waitress in town about Tony. Several called Hughes, and now he's mad as hell."

Aaron shook his head. "Stupid," he said under his breath.

Dudley stood up and put on his hat. "I'm off to do rounds. See you later." He slouched as he left. Aaron thought Duds should just take an early retirement and enjoy the rest of his life.

"And close that door on your way out!" Sheriff Hughes yelled as his office door opened. A thoroughly chastised Deputy Sorenson slunk out and headed for his desk.

"Hey, Frank. Are you okay?" Aaron asked. Even though what Frank did was stupid, he felt bad for him.

"I'm fine," he said, his face turning bright red.

Hughes stuck his head out of his office. "Deputy Jackson! Get in here!"

Aaron sighed. He stood and headed inside Hughes' office, shutting the door behind him. "What's up?"

"Sit down," Hughes said. The sheriff was already sitting behind his desk.

"Okay." Aaron sat.

"Did you hear what that idiot Frank did? Now I have women all over town in an uproar over being accused of having affairs with Tony." Hughes was seething.

"You need to calm down, or your funeral will be next," Aaron said.

"You think this is funny?"

"No, I don't. And what Frank did was stupid. But he's young, and he thought he was helping. Give him a break, okay?"

"I should fire him. Unfortunately, we're already understaffed, and we have some crazy person going around killing people." Hughes ran his hand over his face. "Have you been watching Cassie?"

"Yes. And all she's doing is packing up her mother's house so she can sell it. She's too busy to plan murders," Aaron said.

Hughes leaned on his desk, dropping his elbows on the

paperwork strewn all over it. "Then who's doing it? Huh?"

"Like I said before, Marty and Tony could have had several people who hated them," Aaron said. "Give it time. We'll figure it out."

"Time? Meanwhile, I'm constantly looking over my shoulder, wondering if I'm next."

Aaron sat there quietly. He wouldn't be surprised if there were several people in town who wanted Hughes dead, too.

"Marty's funeral is tomorrow," Aaron said, changing the subject. "Ten a.m. at the mortuary's chapel. His wife isn't coming, so we're in charge."

Hughes shook his head. "I can't believe she won't attend his funeral. Sheesh. You bet she'll be here to sell the house and take whatever money he has, though."

"Yeah. It's a strange situation."

A knock came on the door, and Hughes hollered, "What?"

Frank opened the door and stuck his head inside. "I'm sorry to bother you, sir, but this is important. Rhonda just got a call from Craig Becker's maid." He hesitated.

"And?" Hughes said impatiently.

"She found Mr. Becker dead."

* * *

The paramedics were already at Craig's house when Aaron and Hughes arrived. Aaron had to drive the sheriff there because he was too shaky to take his own car.

"How do you always get here first?" Sheriff Hughes asked Joe and his partner, Claire.

"Rhonda called me. I already checked. Mr. Becker is dead and has been for a while. I think Rhonda already called the coroner, too," Joe said.

Hughes' hands were shaking when he opened the front door and walked inside. Craig's house wasn't as opulent as Marty's, but it was still bigger and nicer than most homes in town. He had a four-bedroom, four bath home which was two stories high and had a fully finished basement where he'd put a pool table. Jason had spent many an evening at Craig's house drinking and shooting pool, especially since Craig's wife left him and remarried two years ago.

"He's sitting at the dining room table," Joe told Hughes and Aaron. "Just sitting there as peacefully as can be excepted, considering the burn marks on his lips."

The Sheriff turned around abruptly. "Burn marks?"

Joe nodded. "I think he drank some type of poison. There's a shot glass on the table. Nothing else. That's for the coroner to determine, though."

Hughes stared at Aaron.

"Do you want me to go inside?" Aaron asked. "You two were close. Maybe seeing him would be too hard."

Sheriff Hughes frowned. "No. I'm the sheriff. I need to see what happened." He turned once more toward the door and stepped over the threshold with Aaron behind him.

Much like Tony's house, there was a nice entryway with a formal living room on the left and the dining room on the right. The staircase curved its way along the wall up to the second floor. Hughes took a right and walked into the dining room. Just as Joe had said, there sat Craig, still in the chair but slumped sideways.

Hughes took a deep breath and walked closer to Craig's body. So did Aaron. Craig's arms hung at his sides, and his head lay on one shoulder. Joe had been right. He looked fine, except for the red marks on his lips and a deeper burn at the corner of his mouth. On the table in front of him was a shot glass with no liquid left in it.

"What the hell happened?" Sheriff Hughes asked. "Do you think he killed himself?"

Aaron studied the scene, then walked through a door into the kitchen. He looked around for any signs of someone else having been there, but the kitchen was spotless. No bottle of liquor and no other shot glass.

"There's no sign that anyone was drinking with him," Aaron called out from the kitchen. "It's spotless in here." He walked back to the dining room. "I have no idea what happened." He turned to Hughes and thought he saw him shiver.

Calvin Evans showed up and studied the scene. His brow wrinkled. "What the hell is going on in this town? Why is everyone dying?"

"You tell me," Sheriff Hughes said.

Calvin took out a notebook and made a few notes. He felt the body, then, without touching it, sniffed the shot glass. "He's been dead since last night. And there had been some type of whiskey in that glass. I can't tell what kind of poison he ingested, but my best guess from the burn marks on his lips is cyanide."

"Cyanide?" Hughes said. "Why the hell would Craig drink cyanide? And where would he get it from?"

"I'm just guessing at this point, Sheriff, so calm down," Calvin said.

"I need to sit down," Hughes said. He left the room and went outside.

Calvin looked at Aaron. "This is a tough one for the Sheriff. I know he and Craig were friends."

Aaron nodded. "He's been friends with all the men who've died. Since high school."

The coroner's brows rose. "Interesting. I had no idea."

"We should bag the glass and all the bottles of whiskey and check them for fingerprints," Aaron said, going into deputy mode. "Will you be able to check his hands to see if he was the one who handled the cyanide or whatever poison that killed him?"

Calvin nodded. "Any liquid poison will leave traces on his fingers. Don't worry, I'll be thorough."

"Thanks, Calvin." Aaron walked to the front door, but then he saw a woman sitting in the living room. He went in there instead. "Hello, ma'am. Are you the woman who found Mr. Becker?"

The middle-aged woman nodded her head. "I'm Elaine Reynolds," she said. "I've been cleaning for Mr. Becker three days a week for about two years now."

Aaron wrote down her name. It made sense since Craig's wife left about two years ago. "Did you find him in the dining room right away?"

She nodded again. "Yes. I was going to head back to the kitchen, down the hallway there," she pointed to the entryway. "But when I saw him sitting, slumped at the table, I thought it was strange. I went to him quickly in case he'd passed out or had a heart attack, but that's when I saw his eyes were open, and he wasn't breathing. I ran out of the room and called the police."

Aaron studied the woman. Her brown hair was cut short, and she was a bit plump. She wore a long top over a pair of knee-length yoga pants and sneakers. She seemed calm, considering she'd found a dead body.

"How well did you know Mr. Becker?" Aaron asked.

"Not well," she said. "He wasn't usually here when I cleaned. And he always paid me on time and never complained. Working for him was easy, almost like working for a ghost."

Aaron's brows rose? "Ghost?"

"Sorry." The woman frowned. "That was a bad choice of words. I just meant that I never saw him, and the checks appeared on the counter each week. And his house wasn't ever dirty. It's like he barely lived here."

Aaron nodded. "I get what you mean." He could relate. His house didn't get very dirty either. "You don't seem too disturbed by finding him dead."

Elaine shrugged. "He's not the first dead person I've found in all the years I've cleaned houses. It's just something that happens."

"I suppose it does," Aaron said. "Did you also wash dishes or put them in the dishwasher as part of your job?"

"Sometimes, yes. He rarely had dirty dishes," she said.

"And you said that you hadn't started working yet before you found Mr. Becker?"

"Yes. I didn't touch anything. I called the police and then came in here to wait," Elaine said.

"Thank you for staying. Your information is helpful," Aaron said, smiling. "Would you mind going down to the sheriff's station and having your fingerprints taken?" When he saw her startled expression, he hurried on. "You're not a suspect. It's routine, so we can eliminate your prints from all the others we may find."

Elaine nodded her head. "I can go right now. I don't have to be at my other client's house for another hour."

"Great. I'll call ahead and let them know why you're there.

Thank you, Elaine. You've been very helpful." Aaron called Rhonda at the office to tell her Elaine was coming in shortly. Then he hung up and walked outside. Hughes was still standing out there talking to Joe and Claire.

"Was that the maid who just left?" Hughes asked. He looked less pale than he had earlier.

"Yes. I already questioned her, and I sent her to the station for fingerprints," Aaron said. "Will we have the forensic team come back for this investigation?"

"I think we can do this scene," Hughes said. "I'll call the Sheriff in the next county and ask him to send his investigative team over for fingerprints. We should also do a walk-through of the house to make sure nothing is disturbed. If someone forced him to drink that poison, then he didn't seem to fight it. The coroner will tell us if there are any defensive marks on Craig."

Aaron nodded. This one was going to be harder to figure out.

"I talked to Craig yesterday around two," Aaron offered up. "I was eating in the bar downtown, and he came in and sat with me."

Hughes frowned. "What was he doing in a bar in the afternoon?"

"I don't know, but he was still working when he had a beer. He seemed nervous. And he kept saying he'd just had a disturbing conversation with someone but didn't say who."

"Interesting," Hughes said, looking thoughtful. "Drive me back to the station, will you? And then go over to the fire station and talk to the guys there. Maybe they saw who talked to him. That may be his killer."

Aaron dropped Hughes off at the station and then drove

the short distance to the fire station. As he walked in through the open garage door, he saw Paul Rearson up on the ladder truck, fixing something.

"Hey, Paul," Aaron called. The young guy waved and stood up.

"What's up?" Paul asked.

Aaron knew the fire crew hadn't yet heard about Craig's death. "Would you round up the people working here today and have them come out here? I need to tell you all something."

Paul looked confused but did as Aaron asked. Three men and a woman came out of the office with Paul and stood, staring expectantly at Aaron.

"Sorry to take you all away from your work, but I needed to tell you something important," Aaron said. "Craig Becker was found dead at his home this morning."

The men's faces showed surprise, and the woman gasped.

"I know how you all feel. It was a shock to the sheriff and me, too. Especially after the deaths of the mayor and district attorney," Aaron said.

Everyone nodded. Even though Aaron knew these people didn't necessarily like Craig, at least they were being respectful.

"I wanted to ask you all if you saw anyone visiting with Craig here at the firehouse yesterday afternoon. I talked to him around two, and he said he'd met with someone who'd upset him."

The woman, who was their receptionist and dispatch operator, spoke up. "A blond woman came inside yesterday afternoon and headed for Becker's office. They spoke for just a couple of minutes, and then she left."

"I saw her too," Paul said. "She was average height with shoulder-length blond hair. She came through the garage and asked about Becker, and I pointed toward the offices. She went inside, and I didn't see her again."

Another man spoke up. "I was talking to Becker when she approached him. He turned so pale I thought he would pass out. But I left to give them privacy."

Aaron's mind was spinning. He knew it must have been Cassie who'd shown up. She was the only person who could have upset Craig that much. And with this many witnesses, there was no way he could hide this from Hughes.

After thanking the fire crew, Aaron drove away. He didn't head to the sheriff's station immediately, though. He had to think this through. As he drove circles around the small town, he decided he had to talk to Cassie. If anything, he had to warn her. Because if news of her visiting the fire station got out, Hughes would definitely bring her in.

Aaron parked in his driveway and took a deep breath. Cassie's car was in her driveway, so she was definitely home. He got out of his car, headed for Cassie's front door, and knocked. After a minute, he heard footsteps walking toward the door, and it opened.

"Why are you here?" she asked sharply. "I thought I made it clear that we weren't friends."

"I'm sorry to bother you, Cass, but I need to talk to you. Can I come in?" Aaron asked.

She shook her head. "No. I don't want to be in a room alone with you."

"This is important," Aaron said. "If I don't talk to you now, Hughes will eventually haul you into the station to talk with you. I don't want that to happen."

She narrowed her eyes. "What is this about?"

"Craig Becker was found dead this morning."

"So? What does that have to do with me?" Cassie asked.

Aaron was taken aback that she showed no surprise over Craig's death. "I know you visited him yesterday at the fire station. There are witnesses."

"Then the witnesses will tell you that Craig was very much alive when I left," Cassie said, pushing the door closed.

Aaron placed his polished shoe in the door before it closed. "Cass. I know you were at Marty's and Tony's houses the days that they died. And now there's proof you visited Craig at work. If I dig enough, I'm sure I'll find evidence that you were at Craig's house last night. So, do you want to talk now? Or do you want to wait for Hughes to pull you in?"

Cassie sighed and opened the door again. "Fine. Let's talk."

CHAPTER THIRTEEN

There was no way Cassie was letting Aaron inside the house, so she stepped out onto the stoop, and they sat there just as they had the other night.

"So, ask me your questions," Cassie said curtly.

"Why were you at the fire station yesterday?" Aaron asked. He pulled out his notepad and pen to write down her answers, even though he had a feeling she wouldn't give him any.

"That's none of your business," Cassie said. "Next."

Aaron sighed. "Whatever you said to Craig, it upset him. He came into the bar downtown where I was eating lunch and was really freaked out. He said he'd had a weird conversation with someone."

"Did he say it was me?" Cassie asked, looking hard at Aaron.

"No. But then I found out today you'd been at the fire station. Workers there saw you. This time, it can't be hidden," Aaron said, getting more nervous by the second. The last thing he wanted was for Hughes to have an excuse to arrest Cassie.

"Hidden? What do you mean by that?" Cassie asked.

"I haven't told Jason yet that I saw you at Marty's and Tony's houses right before they died. I even risked my job by erasing the video at Tony's house showing you coming and going that evening. Cass," Aaron sounded desperate. "If Jason finds out you were at both places and that you visited Craig at his work, he'll finally have a reason to blame these deaths on you."

Cassie stood. "I never asked you to risk your job or hide anything. I don't care who knows that I spoke to each of those guys before they died. They were all very much alive when I left them. I have nothing to hide."

"Were you at Craig's house last night?" Aaron asked.

"Yes. I went there at seven fifteen and left by seven-thirty. So what."

Craig stood and stared into Cassie's eyes. "Don't you get it, Cassie? You've been at the scene of each murder during the timeframe when the murders occurred. If Hughes finds out what I know, that will be it. He's been looking for a reason to pin these murders on you and to get rid of you. Now, he may have what he wants."

Cassie took a step back and crossed her arms. "He has no proof I did anything. Have my fingerprints shown up at the crime scenes? Did anyone else except you see me at any of the houses? It seems to me that you're trying to tie me to the murders, not Jason."

"Cassie. Let me help you, please. I know you didn't kill those men, but proving you didn't is going to be difficult. Maybe you should leave now. Just pack up your mother's car with the boxes you have ready and leave. I can ship the others to you. Please. I don't want Jason to arrest you for murder."

"That's always your answer, isn't it? Run away." Cassie shook her head. "Well, this time, I'm not running. I haven't done anything, and no one is going to arrest me. Jason knows if he comes near me, I'll tell the world about the night he and his crew attacked me. And I also know how to prove it. The hospital did a rape kit on me that night. It will implicate all four men in the attack. And I wasn't deaf that night. I heard you talk about the other girls they killed."

Aaron's eyes widened. "You know about them?"

"Yes. And I'll bet those poor women are buried on that property somewhere. If I go to the authorities and tell them what I know, then that will prove it happened to me, too. Except I lived."

Aaron's shoulders slumped as he sat down again on the stoop. "You're right. That's all it would take. And I know where the bodies are buried because I was there when they buried them."

Cassie couldn't believe what he'd said. "Wait! You, an officer of the law, know where the dead women are buried? And you've never turned Jason or the others in. That makes you as guilty as they are." Cassie was disgusted by this news. Knowing it happened was one thing, but knowing where the girls were buried and keeping it to himself all these years was too much.

Aaron looked at her. "Maybe that's exactly what we should do. You could go to the police with what you know, and Jason will rot in prison for the rest of his life. It's the perfect revenge."

Cassie backed up another step. "I'm not looking for revenge. And I don't want to be a part of any plot trying to destroy someone—even someone as disgusting as Jason." Cassie was through with this conversation. She didn't want to spend another moment around Aaron. "You need to leave. And I don't want you near me again, do you hear? Leave!"

Aaron stood, his expression pained. "I'm just trying to help you," he said pitifully.

"Help me? Like the night I was attacked? No, thank you. Leave. Get off my property and stay off!" Cassie screamed at Aaron.

"Okay. I'm leaving. I never meant to upset you. Please don't be angry with me."

"Leave!" Cassie yelled. She ran past him, up the steps, and through the door, slamming it shut. The lock clicked.

Cassie stood with her back against the door for several minutes until her heart rate slowed. She couldn't believe the things Aaron had said. She had always thought he was a good guy who'd been dragged into a bad situation. But now she didn't know what to think. Had he known what the guys were going to do to her that night twenty years ago and brought her there on purpose? He'd already known about the other two women. Was he just as guilty as they were?

"I need to get out of here," she said aloud. She had to pack up the house fast and leave for good. This place was nothing but trouble, and it was time to go.

CHAPTER FOURTEEN

Aaron was shaking so badly by the time he slid back into his service car that he had to sit there for a few minutes to calm down. His conversation with Cassie hadn't gone as planned. And once he'd lost control of it, he felt like he'd lost control of everything. Did he really tell Cassie that he knew where the other bodies were buried? Why had he done that? And what if she went through with her threat to tell the authorities? No matter what happened, he had to make sure Jason didn't know Cassie had been around Marty, Tony, and Craig before they died. Otherwise, all hell would break loose.

Aaron drove back to the sheriff's station and was surprised to see the television vans were back and people were milling around the front of the building. He drove around to the back and walked in the door.

"How the hell do they find out this stuff so fast?" Sheriff Hughes was yelling as Aaron walked into the office area. "And where were you again?" His anger was directed at Aaron. "You keep disappearing."

Aaron shoved his hands in his pants pockets so Hughes

wouldn't see them shaking. "I went to the fire station to ask a few questions like you told me to."

"Well? Did they have any news?"

"Nothing substantial," Aaron said. "Just a regular day there yesterday." He wondered how long it would be before Hughes learned the truth.

"Come into my office," Hughes said, heading in that direction.

Aaron followed and shut the door behind him.

Hughes sat down behind his desk and heaved a heavy sigh. "We have the media on our ass again, and I have to do another press conference. They're now asking if we have a serial killer here. Or if the murders are related." He stared hard at Aaron. "What if someone starts talking about the four of us being friends in high school, and they put two and two together?"

Aaron frowned. "No one knows what happened out at the cabin except the dead guys and us. How could anyone learn anything?"

"We don't know if Marty, Tony, or Craig ever told anyone—or bragged to anyone about the murders," Hughes said. "And Cassie knows."

Aaron rolled his eyes. "Stop blaming it on Cassie. She could have pressed charges decades ago. She didn't. Leave her out of it."

Hughes opened his bottom drawer and pulled out the whiskey bottle and glass. He poured himself a large portion of the amber liquid and took a long drink.

"That's not going to help, Jason," Aaron said.

"Really? Well, you should join me because, by my estimation, we're next."

"You know, there's still the possibility that all the men

killed themselves, and the coroner got it wrong," Aaron said. "We could just say that's what happened like you suggested before, and the case will be closed."

Hughes set his glass on his desk and stared at Aaron. "And why would they do that?"

"All three men had failed marriages. Tony cheated on his wife with multiple women. Maybe they were unhappy with their lives. Maybe they all did something in the past that came back to haunt them. There could be multiple reasons why each of them would kill themselves."

Hughes took another long drink. "So, is that what you're going to say when you find me dead? That it was suicide. Because I can bet you I'm next."

"You've got to stop drinking like that," Aaron said, shaking his head.

"Why? I think I'd rather be drunk than sober when the Grim Reaper comes for me," Hughes said.

Aaron stood up. "Fine. Drink. But by this evening, you'd better be sober because you'll have to tell the reporters something. You can tell them there's a murderer in town or that they committed suicide. It's up to you." He headed for the door.

"Hey! Where are you going?" Hughes yelled.

"I'm going to Craig's house to look around for any evidence, and then I'll do my regular rounds. Believe me. I'm as tired of all of this as you are." Aaron shut the door behind him and walked through the office and out to his car. He knew he wouldn't find any evidence at Craig's house, but he had to go through the motions. He thought he knew who killed the men, and he was sure the murderer had left everything clean.

* * *

Sheriff Hughes had a press conference at five o'clock that evening, looking more sober than he really was.

"As you all have heard, Craig Becker has passed away today, becoming the third death in the past several days in our small town," Hughes said. "He was found this morning by his maid. After an investigation at his home, we have found no evidence to suggest it was a murder. But until the autopsy is complete, the investigation is still open."

Suddenly, flashbulbs went off, and microphones were shoved in his face. Aaron watched it all, standing at attention behind Hughes. Deputy Sorenson stood beside Aaron.

Hughes raised his hands to ward off the bright lights, and the microphones pulled back. "As for the deaths of Martin Kroger and Anthony Wiles, they, too, are still under investigation. However, in all the cases, suicide could still be a factor. Thank you." He was about to turn around when a woman screamed out at him.

"Is it true all the men were your friends in high school?"

Sheriff Hughes turned toward the voice. "Yes. We all went to high school together, as did many other people in town. It's a small town. We all know each other."

"Are you afraid you're next?" she called out.

Hughes frowned. "Why would I be next?" he asked. "That's ridiculous."

"The mayor, the district attorney, and the fire chief are now dead. Don't you think the sheriff would be next?" the woman asked.

Aaron watched as all eyes turned to Hughes. He saw the sheriff begin to shake.

"No! I don't believe this nonsense," Hughes bellowed. "Go

do your jobs, and let me do mine." He turned and stormed into the sheriff's station.

"Oh, boy," Frank said beside Aaron. "He'll be yelling at us now."

This made Aaron chuckle despite the brevity of the moment. "I think you're right."

By the time Aaron and Frank walked into the office, Hughes had already locked himself in his private office.

"I'm clocking out," Aaron told Frank. "I've been here all day. Dudley is out doing rounds. I suggest you get a good night's sleep too. Tomorrow is Marty's funeral."

"Oh, yeah. That's right." Frank shook his head. "One of three that we need to attend. It's going to be a rough couple of weeks."

Aaron nodded. He waved at the night desk clerk as he left the station. Driving in his own car, he passed the front of the sheriff's station and saw that several of the news vans were still parked there. *What do they think they'll get this late at night? Another murder?* Aaron shuddered at the thought of that. One more to go, he thought. If this was someone seeking revenge, then Hughes would be dead soon, too.

He parked in his driveway, noting that Cassie's car was still in hers. He'd better keep an eye on her car, just to make sure she doesn't make any more nightly visits. Even though he was ninety-nine percent sure she didn't kill the three men, he still needed to keep an eye on her.

As he walked into his house, a thought occurred to him. Could the families of the other two women killed somehow have found out that Hughes and his friends had killed their family member? It would be a long shot, but it was a thought.

After making dinner, Aaron sat down at his laptop, popped

open a beer, and typed in 'Missing women around Morgan Falls, MN.' He wondered why he'd never thought to do this before. He'd never seen the women's faces, only knew that Hughes and Marty had picked them up on the side of the road somewhere between Morgan Falls and the next town. By the time Aaron helped bury the women, they were wrapped in a tarp. He'd been disgusted helping Hughes dispose of the bodies, but as always, Jason had found a way to con him into helping.

Ten names popped up on the screen. That surprised Aaron. Five were the wrong years, three were too young, but two of the women went missing within a year of each other, around the same time as Hughes picked them up. One year apart. Almost exactly one year apart. Why hadn't the press or the local authorities in the other town noticed that and questioned it?

Tiffany Wexley was nineteen and from the town twenty miles away from Morgan Falls. She was tall and slender with black hair and brown eyes. Her boyfriend had kicked her out of his car after they'd had a fight and left her to walk home on the dark road.

Aaron stared at her picture. "Stupid boyfriend," he said aloud. She was exactly the type of girl Jason would pick up.

The other woman was Amanda Glass. She was twenty years old at the time and blond with blue eyes. Her car had broken down on the deserted road, and her cell phone battery was dead. The only reason they knew this was because her phone was found in her car. She must have started walking back to town and that was when Jason would have picked her up.

Disgusting.

Both cases were never solved because it was as if the girls had vanished from the face of the planet.

Closing his computer, Aaron drank down the last of his beer and headed to bed. His hatred of Jason and the other guys had grown even more. They had gotten what they deserved, as far as he was concerned.

* * *

The next morning, Aaron arrived at work at nine o'clock. He figured he'd be driving Hughes to the funeral, so he went in early. Frank was already there, but since Duds had worked the night shift, he'd gone home to sleep.

"Has Sheriff Hughes come in yet?" Aaron asked Rhonda.

She shook her head. "I haven't seen him."

Frowning, Aaron went to Hughes' office and opened the door. There lay Hughes on the sofa, out cold, with his service revolver lying on his huge belly.

"Sheesh!" Aaron said, closing the door. He glanced at the desk and saw that Hughes had polished off the bottle of whiskey.

"Jason! Wake up!" Aaron said sharply.

Hughes sat up and swung his pistol toward Aaron. Luckily, the safety was on.

"Christ, Aaron. What the hell? I could have shot you." Hughes slid his legs over the side of the sofa and set his pistol on the end table. "Shit. My head aches."

"I can't believe you slept here," Aaron said with disgust. "Or, to be exact, passed out here."

"There was no way I was going home," Hughes said. "I didn't want to be dead by morning."

"You smell like whiskey," Aaron said. "We have to be at Marty's funeral in forty-five minutes."

"Crap!" Hughes stood, then sat down again. "My head is pounding."

"Do you have another uniform here?" Aaron asked. "You can shower in the locker room and change. We have to get going. It won't look good if you don't attend the mayor's funeral, and the press will be there."

Hughes sighed. "Fine. Get me some coffee, and I'll go clean up." He stood again, then slowly made his way out of the office and toward the locker room.

"He looks terrible," Frank said as Aaron poured a cup of coffee for Hughes.

"Yeah," Aaron said. "But he'd better look sober and alert by the time we head to the funeral."

Since there was no family attending, Aaron, Hughes, and Frank sat in the chapel's front row. The room was packed with people who'd grown up with Marty, as well as his co-workers at city hall and many others who'd known him through the years. The press hadn't been allowed inside, so they were camped outside, waiting for everyone to walk out.

As the minister spoke, Calvin, who sat behind them, leaned forward and whispered to Hughes, "Suicide? Are you really trying to dismiss all the deaths as suicides?"

Aaron glared at Calvin. This wasn't the place to discuss this.

Hughes made a half turn toward Calvin. "We don't know for sure yet, but it could be. You haven't really proved otherwise."

Everyone stood to sing *How Great Thou Art,* but Calivn kept talking. "You know as well as I do that Marty didn't choke himself before he was hanged. And Tony didn't shoot himself."

"Shh!" Aaron said to Calvin. "This isn't the place for this."

Calvin shook his head and stared straight ahead.

After the service, they all went into the reception room for lunch. Calvin followed Hughes around.

"Listen, Calvin," Hughes finally said, turning in the line for food to stare at him. "It was just an observation. After we investigate everything, I'll make my determination."

"Investigate," Calvin said, sneering. "Is that what you call your Laural and Hardy operation? You couldn't solve a murder if the killer slapped you in the face."

Aaron watched as Hughes' face turned a deep red. The guy was going to have a coronary right there.

"Calvin. Please," Aaron said, pulling him aside. "Just let it go for now. Three of Jason's friends are dead. Give him a break, okay?"

Calvin nodded and stalked out of the room.

Hughes loaded his plate with sandwiches, noodle salad, and three different kinds of bars. Then he headed for the back corner of the room and sat down. Aaron joined him.

"We have to figure out who's killing people—quickly," Hughes told Aaron. "I still think Cassie has something to do with it. Maybe she hired someone."

Aaron sighed. He pushed his plate of food aside because his appetite had left him. "Give it a rest, will you, Jason? Cassie had nothing to do with these guys dying." He watched as Hughes stuffed his face with sandwiches. "Have you ever considered that the murders might be connected to the other two women who died?" he whispered.

Hughes' head snapped up. "Not here!" he said.

After the luncheon, Aaron, Frank, and Hughes followed the hearse to the cemetery along with a few other people to attend the interment. They stood there as the minister said a last prayer, and then everyone slowly walked away. But Hughes remained as the groundskeeper placed Marty's urn in the small hole and began shoveling dirt over it.

"That's an awfully small hole for such a big guy," Hughes said.

Aaron had stayed, too, but Frank had headed out on his rounds. "This is what it all comes down to," Aaron said.

The two walked down the row of headstones. Hughes stopped at an ornate black marble headstone. "My father," he said. "My dad always had to have the best, even in death."

Aaron nodded respectfully. His father's headstone wasn't nearly as big and gaudy. Everything about Aaron's life was smaller than everyone else's.

Hughes turned to Aaron. "What did you mean about the murders being connected to the other women?"

"I just thought that maybe one of the women's families figured out what happened, and now a brother or father is getting revenge," Aaron said. "I looked up missing women and found them online."

"Why?" Hughes asked, irritated. "Why would you do that? No one knows about them or what happened to them. Didn't you think that looking them up online might lead someone to you? People can trace anything these days."

"I doubt if anyone is tracing my computer, Jason," he said. "It was just a thought."

"I need to go home and get some sleep," Hughes said. "Drop me off there, okay?"

Aaron drove Hughes to the edge of town where his house sat on property his parents once owned. Years ago, Jason's father had given him five acres and helped pay to build his house. It wasn't fancy by any means, but it was nice and in a peaceful setting.

As Aaron drove up Hughes' long driveway, he asked, "Whatever happened to that property where your father's hunting cabin was?"

Hughes frowned. "After the cabin burned to the ground, my dad sold the land to the farmer next door to it. Dad thought I accidentally burned it down while we were all out there drinking, and he just got rid of it."

"Hm." Aaron stopped in front of Jason's house. "Have you ever walked along the river there? You know. Just to make sure the graves weren't disturbed."

"Why?" Hughes asked angrily. "Obviously, if the farmer had ever dug up the graves, it would have been reported." He eyed Aaron. "Why are you bringing all this up?"

Aaron shrugged. "Just thinking out loud, I guess. Someone is behind these murders. It's not too far of a stretch to think one of the missing girls' relatives could be the murderer."

"Stop talking about this stuff," Hughes said, getting out of the car. "I mean it. It's ancient history. Keep your stupid ideas to yourself." He slammed the door and walked toward his house.

Aaron slowly pulled out of the driveway. He was not going to let it go. If anything, he'd keep digging up more information. Maybe the past would bury Jason after all.

CHAPTER FIFTEEN

Cassie had worked all day packing up her mother's clothes and going through everything in her closet. This was taking so much longer than she'd thought. Halfway through the day, she wondered if she should tell her husband to fly out and help her. His clear head and analytical mind would help her make decisions faster, and they could get this done in half the time.

She just didn't want him to be infected by this horrible little town.

Cassie opened the big garage door for fresh air while she stacked boxes for storage. She was setting another box in the back of her mother's car to take to Goodwill tomorrow when she saw Aaron's car pull into his driveway.

Stay away, she thought as he got out of his car. *Stay away from me.* Unfortunately, her thoughts hadn't been strong enough because he headed straight for her.

"Go away," Cassie said, her finger already on the garage door button.

"Wait! Cassie. I know you don't want me around, but can I talk to you for a moment?"

Cassie knew she should say no. She knew she should tell him to leave and shut the door. But then she decided they were out in the open, so she supposed it was safe to talk with him.

"What?" she asked.

"Something occurred to me last night, and I wanted to run it by you," he said. "I have a theory about the murders."

"Good for you. Not my problem," she said

"No. Wait. I looked up the two women who were murdered by Jason and his friends all those years ago. Actually, I looked up missing women and narrowed it down to the two. I never actually saw them," Aaron said.

"Why are you telling me this?"

"I wondered if maybe a family member of one of them could have learned the truth and is killing the guys," Aaron said.

Cassie stopped a moment and thought about that. "Wouldn't they have just gone to the authorities?"

"Maybe. But maybe they thought revenge would be better than trying to catch four guys twenty years later."

"Did the guys brag about what they did?" Cassie asked, feeling disgusted just talking about them. "Otherwise, there'd be no way for anyone to know."

Aaron sighed. "I'm not sure. But it was a thought."

"Aaron. Stop getting me involved in this," Cassie said angrily. "I don't care who murdered those men or if they committed suicide. They deserved it, and so does Jason. But that's not up to me or you. And I'm not staying here long enough to learn the truth."

Aaron looked at the car as if noticing the many boxes for the first time. "Is that the stuff you're taking with you?"

"No. This is for Goodwill. I've decided to take only the

stuff that means the most to me and sell the rest. I took a bunch of boxes of home items and dishes to the antique store today and then I'm taking these boxes tomorrow. After that, I'm packing up and leaving."

"Tomorrow?" Aaron asked.

"Yes. Tomorrow." Cassie frowned at him. "You're the one who told me to get out of here as soon as possible."

Aaron nodded. "Right. Yeah. That's a good idea. It's just that I'll miss you not being next door anymore."

"What? I haven't lived next door for twenty years, Aaron. Listen. I don't know what's going on in that brain of yours, but please leave me alone. I just want to go home and back to my own life."

"I don't blame you for that," Aaron said. "Well, it was great seeing you again, even if you can't stand the sight of me. I'm so sorry for everything that happened to you. I hope you can put it all behind you."

"I already have, Aaron," Cassie said. "And once I no longer have ties to this town, it will be permanent."

Aaron turned to leave, then turned back.

"What now?" Cassie asked, sighing.

"Why did you go see Marty, Tony, and Craig before they died? Could your visit to each of them have caused them to commit suicide?"

Cassie deflated. She was so tired of all this. "I saw them for personal reasons," she said. "And no. Each of them was fine when I left. Except for Marty, who was very drunk. If they killed themselves, it had nothing to do with me."

"Will you be visiting Jason before you go?" Aaron asked. "Because I have to warn you, he's scared shitless and keeps his gun on him all the time."

She shook her head. "No. I don't need to. I have what I came for."

Aaron nodded, then walked to his house.

Cassie sighed, relieved. One more night and she was out of here. Thank God.

CHAPTER SIXTEEN

I have what I came for. Aaron thought about Cassie's words all night. What had she meant by them? What had she needed from the three guys that she didn't need from Jason or even him?

As Aaron sat in his house, he thought about his life. Cassie had a life to go back to, but what did he have? He had a job where he worked with the man he'd hated since that night long ago. He had no wife, no girlfriend, and no children. Of course, that was his own fault because the only woman he'd ever really loved left a long time ago. And she was leaving again for the last time tomorrow.

It was time he changed his life. It was time to put a plan in motion.

The next morning, Aaron got up early, dressed in his uniform, and drove out to Jason's house.

"What are you doing here so early?" Jason asked, looking blurry-eyed. It was obvious he'd been drinking all night again.

"I just got a call from Rhonda. The guy who owns your father's river property called," Aaron said. "He decided to clear a spot by the river to build a house for himself, and you'll never guess what he found?"

Hughes' eyes grew wide. "Are you shitting me?"

"No. And we'd better get out there before anyone else does. If there's any incriminating evidence, we need to grab it before the coroner or a forensic team is called," Aaron said.

"There shouldn't be any evidence after all these years," Hughes said.

"What about the tarps they were buried in? What about DNA on clothing? They can get DNA from a stain from thousands of years ago. It won't be that hard to do it from twenty years ago."

"Shit!" Hughes ran to his bedroom and put on his uniform. He was dressed and ready to go in five minutes. They got in Aaron's service car and headed out of town toward the property.

"That's insane that he'd find their bodies the day after we were talking about them," Hughes said, still looking half-awake.

"It's a coincidence, that's for sure," Aaron said. "And a terrible one at that. We should have buried them deeper. Or buried them on another property. Crap!" Aaron shook his head. "That property is legally connected to your family. Why had we been so stupid?"

"I never thought my father would sell the property," Hughes said. "He loved hunting there." He sat silent for a moment. "The best we can do is mess up the dig site and get our DNA all over it. Since we'll be there first, the forensic team will just think we fucked up the scene."

"Yeah. Because a semen stain on the girls' clothing will be considered just a fuck-up," Aaron said.

"Good God! What are we going to do?" Hughes was shaking.

"We'll just have to take it as it comes," Aaron said. "I know my DNA isn't anywhere on those girls."

"Well, lucky you," Hughes said snidely.

Aaron turned left off the highway onto the wooded property. The narrow road hadn't changed in twenty years. The trees towered overhead, drawing long shadows over the car.

"I don't remember this road being so spooky," Hughes said, his eyes darting around.

"I do," Aaron said. "That last night I brought Cassie, she was shivering from how creepy everything looked. If I'd listened to her protests, she would never have left town, and she wouldn't hate me."

"And she wouldn't have married you or stayed anyway," Hughes said. "Cassie was the smart one. She was determined to leave this town even before we attacked her."

Aaron glared at Hughes. "You don't know that. You were so self-centered then; you wouldn't have even thought about what Cassie wanted."

"Yeah, yeah. I was a jerk. But at least I knew what I was. You hung out with a jerk and his friends. What does that say about you?" Hughes said.

Suddenly, the trees opened up into a clearing, and standing in front of them was a cabin.

Hughes gasped. "What the hell? Why is that cabin here?" His head spun back and forth. "Isn't this the exact spot it was before?"

Aaron parked the car in front of the cabin and stared at it. "Maybe the owner built it. It is the perfect place for a cabin since there's a clearing here." He opened his door and took off his seatbelt.

"What are you doing?" A wide-eyed Hughes asked.

"I'm going to see if someone is around," Aaron said. He grinned. "Why? Are you scared?"

Deep wrinkles formed around Hughes' downturned mouth. "Asshole." He unsnapped his seatbelt and opened the car door. "I doubt anyone lives here. It must be a hunting shack."

Aaron walked up onto the porch and stared through the only window on the right-hand side. "I don't see anyone." He went to the door and knocked.

"It's uncanny," Hughes said, looking amazed. "It looks exactly like my dad's cabin."

Aaron tried the doorknob, and it turned, so he opened the door.

"What are you doing? You can't just walk into someone's place," Hughes said.

"No one's here. Who will know?" Aaron walked inside. "Coming?"

Hughes took a deep breath and walked in behind Aaron. "Oh, my God! It's exactly like my dad's cabin," Hughes said. A stone fireplace stood on the center wall, and there was a sofa and rug just like the ones that had been there years ago. He turned to Aaron. "What the hell is going on here?" he asked.

Aaron grinned. "Welcome to hell."

* * *

Just before noon, Aaron called Rhonda at the sheriff's station and asked her to call Cassandra Sanders and have her come in to be fingerprinted. "Sheriff Hughes insisted on it," Aaron said, sounding annoyed.

"Where is the Sheriff?" Rhonda asked. "I haven't seen him all day."

"He's at home, sick," Aaron said. "More like hungover, but you didn't hear it from me." Aaron laughed.

Rhonda chuckled. "Yeah. I guess he's pretty freaked out by everything that's been going on. If you come in, be sure to park in the back. The press is still hanging out in front of the station."

"Thanks, Rhonda. I'll be in there soon." Aaron hung up. He was personally going to take care of Cassie.

* * *

Cassie had just come home from making a trip to Goodwill when her phone buzzed. She frowned upon seeing the call was from the sheriff's office. "Hello?" she said, sounding more annoyed than she'd meant to. She just wanted to pack up her car and get out of there for good.

"Cassandra Sanders?" The woman on the other line asked. "This is Rhonda Jorgensen from the Morgan Falls Sheriff's Department. I'm sorry to bother you, but Sheriff Hughes has requested you come down to be fingerprinted."

"What?" Cassie was shocked. "Why?"

"I'm not sure why," the woman said. "I suppose since it's just a request, it's to eliminate your prints from any others found."

Eliminate my prints, Cassie thought. Had Aaron told Jason she'd been at the houses after all? "Okay," Cassie said. "Is Deputy Jackson there? I don't want to meet with Sheriff Hughes alone."

"Yes, ma'am. Deputy Jackson is on his way here. And you might want to park in the back. There's press all over the front entrance."

Cassie sighed. "I'll be in shortly," she said before hanging up.

They won't find my fingerprints in any of the houses, she thought. *I made sure of that.*

Glancing at the boxes she'd placed in the garage, she decided to pack up the car after she was finished at the sheriff's station. And then, she was out of here.

Cassie arrived at the sheriff's station, and just as the woman had said, there were media vans all over in front. She rounded the corner and pulled into the back area. She was relieved to see that Aaron's car was already there. The last thing she wanted was to be in a room alone with Jason.

Cassie entered through the back door, where Aaron, dressed in his uniform, was waiting.

"Sorry you had to come in to do this," he said, looking apologetic. "Hughes is trying to pin the murders on you. This is the only way to make sure he can't."

"Does this mean I can't leave town?" Cassie asked, suddenly scared she'd be stuck here even longer.

"No, not at all. There's no evidence against you. In fact, I think they committed suicide. This is just to eliminate you from possible suspects."

"Okay. Let's get this over quickly, then. I'm leaving town after this," Cassie said.

"Just come in here," Aaron said, opening a door in the hall-way. "It'll only take a second."

Cassie walked into the room ahead of him and then realized something was wrong. This was just a janitor's closet. Before she could turn around, a rag was placed over her nose and mouth. She struggled fiercely, but Aaron held on tightly. Then, everything went dark.

Cassie slowly came awake, still smelling the sweet scent of the damp cloth that had been held over her nose. As the haze faded, she realized she was lying in the back seat of a car—her car. Taking a few deep breaths, she tried to sit up, and that's when she saw Aaron sitting behind the wheel.

"Sorry I had to do that," Aaron said, turning so she could see his face. "But I knew you wouldn't come with me voluntarily."

"What are you doing?" she asked. Her speech was slurred.

"I'm not going to hurt you," he said quickly. "And no one else will hurt you either. Not this time, I promise. In fact, you're going to finally get what you've wanted all these years."

The fog drifting inside Cassie's brain was clearing. As she looked into Aaron's eyes, she saw something that scared her. Something evil.

"I'm going to help you out of the car now," Aaron said. "Please don't fight me. We're too many miles out of town for you to run." He stepped out of the car and opened the back door. Cassie tried to scooch out of the seat, but her head was spinning. Aaron offered his hand, and she reluctantly accepted it.

The sun was fading in the sky when Cassie stood up beside Aaron. "How long have I been out?" she asked, gazing around. They were in the woods. Panic rose inside her. *Where were they?*

"I'm afraid that stuff knocked you out for a couple of hours. Sorry," Aaron said. "But we're here now, together, and that's all that matters."

Cassie frowned at him. "Where is here?"

Aaron turned her around, and her eyes grew wide. She was standing in front of the cabin of her nightmares. She gasped, and if she hadn't felt like vomiting, she would have screamed.

"It's exactly the same, isn't it?" Aaron said proudly. "Built on the exact spot where the other cabin burned down." He was staring at the building with admiration. Cassie wondered what kind of nightmare she'd just been dragged into.

"Take me home," Cassie said forcefully. "Now! I don't know what you're up to, Aaron, but this isn't funny. I want to go home."

Aaron looked hurt. "But you haven't even seen the inside yet. Or your surprise. Believe me, you're going to thank me after this is over. I promise." His hand grasped her upper arm harder than necessary. "Let's go inside."

As Aaron dragged her up the stairs onto the porch, she forced herself not to panic. *Be nice. Speak sweetly,* she thought.

"Aaron. Thank you for sharing this with me, but I really have to leave now. My husband is waiting for me to come home. He knows I'll be there in three days. I really need to get on the road. I promise I won't tell anyone about what happened tonight."

Aaron stared at her, looking confused. "Nothing's happened yet." He opened the front door and pulled her across the threshold. Cassie gasped. The place looked exactly like the cabin from graduation night. Same fireplace. Same sofa. Same lit oil lamps. Same rug on the floor. But there was one difference. Sitting, tied to a dining table chair in the middle of the room, was Jason.

"What the hell is going on?" Jason yelled, struggling to get loose from the ropes. "Let me go, Aaron!"

Aaron laughed.

Cassie pulled away from Aaron and moved a step back. Jason's face was black and blue, and his pupils were dilated. For a big guy like Jason not to be able to break free of his ropes, he must have been drugged.

"Aaron. What's going on? Why is Jason tied up?" Cassie asked. Her eyes darted around, looking for a way to escape.

Aaron turned to Cassie and smiled that evil grin again. His eyes were wide. *He's insane,* Cassie thought. *He's completely lost it.*

"I did this for you," Aaron said lovingly. "The others who hurt you are dead. And now you can get revenge on the worst of them. It's your turn to kill Jason."

Cassie's heart beat faster. How in the hell was she going to get out of this alive?

"You built this cabin to get revenge on Jason?" Cassie asked. She had to stall for time until she could think of a way out of there.

Aaron nodded proudly. "I did. I bought this property from the farmer next door years ago, then built this cabin. I hoped that someday, somehow, I'd be able to give you a chance to have your revenge. And now, here we are." He reached under a sofa cushion and pulled out a pistol. Cassie knew it wasn't his service revolver because it looked smaller.

"What the hell are you going to do with that?" Jason asked, his eyes widening.

"Shut up!" Aaron yelled at him. "Or I'll beat the hell out of you again."

"Easy, since I'm tied up, you coward," Jason retorted.

Aaron's face grew red. He took two steps toward Jason and hit him across the face with the revolver. Cassie screamed as the chair tipped over, and Jason's head hit the floor hard.

"Don't worry about him," Aaron told her harshly, then calmed down. "He's the monster, remember? He's the one who brutalized you that night. He doesn't deserve to live."

Cassie backed up another step. "Why do you have that?" she asked, nodding at the gun.

Aaron seemed to have forgotten the pistol in his hand, then

looked at it like he was surprised. "This? Do you know my father gave this to me on my eighteenth birthday? Jason and I were the first ones to use it, hunting grouse, on this very property. The night the guys attacked you, I remembered I had it in my glove compartment. I wanted to storm in here and kill them all to save you." Tears filled his eyes. "But I couldn't. Four against one, even with a gun, I probably would have lost. I hated myself for years knowing I could have done something but was too afraid to do it."

"Coward," Jason's muffled voice said from where he lay.

"Shut up!" Aaron bellowed. He turned to Cassie. "I decided to kill myself instead." Aaron placed the pistol to his temple.

Cassie gasped. "Don't!"

Aaron smiled as he slowly lowered the pistol to his side. "I knew you loved me. I knew it. And that's why I didn't shoot myself. It wouldn't have changed anything. And thank God I didn't. Because I was able to pull you out of the burning cabin and save your life."

"I knew it," Jason said from the floor. "I knew you saved her."

Aaron stalked over next to Jason and pointed the gun at his head. "One more word, and I'll blow your brains out. Just like I did Tony's."

"You killed Tony?" Cassie asked. She was shocked that Aaron could kill anyone. But she wanted to distract him from shooting Jason.

"Of course I did," Aaron said, moving back toward her. "For you. I killed them all for you."

Cassie's stomach lurched. "Why? Why did you kill them?"

"Because they hurt you," Aaron said gently. "Because they ruined your life." He walked back to where Jason lay and easily heaved the chair up so Jason was sitting upright again. "I want you to see and hear everything," he said in Jason's face. "I want you to see the pistol barrel when it's between your eyes."

Jason was breathing heavily, all the bravado knocked out of him.

"Why, Aaron? I never wanted revenge. Why would you do all of this?" Cassie asked. She was disgusted that he killed the men for her.

Aaron stared at her, looking confused. "It's what I thought you wanted."

"No," Cassie said. "I never wanted that."

"I thought that was why you were at each of their houses before they each died," Aaron said. "Were you blackmailing them?"

"She was at their houses?" Jason asked, surprised. "Did she kill them!"

Cassie took another step away from Aaron. "No, I didn't kill them. Marty, Tony, and Craig were all alive when I left them."

"Then why were you there?" Aaron asked.

Cassie looked around. She had no idea how to get out of this mess. She'd have to keep Aaron talking. "I asked them for a DNA sample," she finally said.

"What?" Jason's face was scrunched up. "So you could prosecute them?"

"No," Cassie said. She took a deep breath. "So I could determine which of you was the father of my son."

Both men looked shocked.

"You have a son?" Aaron asked.

Cassie nodded. "Yes. As a result of that horrible night. I almost terminated the pregnancy, then changed my mind. And

I'm glad I did. He isn't anything like any of you. He's bright, sweet, and kind. I don't even know why I bothered to try to find out which of you is his father."

"A son," Aaron said dreamily. "I could have taken care of you. If only you'd come home, I would have married you and taken care of both of you."

Cassie shook her head. "There was no way I wanted anyone in this town to know I'd had him. There'd be too many questions. And he deserved better than this place."

"Wait," Jason said. "You never came to me to get DNA."

She turned to him. "I never wanted to be alone with you. I got your DNA from a glass at the diner the day you freaked out and ran out of the place."

"Ah. It's all making sense now," Aaron said. He grinned. "And I did what you didn't have the nerve to do. I got rid of the scum bags."

Cassie stared at him. "Have you been planning this all along? All these years?"

He smiled. "I've thought about it for years. That's why I built the cabin. At some point, I was going to get them all here and burn it down with them inside. But then you came home, and I thought up a different plan. When I saw you leaving Marty's house that morning, it gave me an idea. That's when I decided to kill them one at a time and watch the others squirm."

"Jesus, Aaron," Jason said. "Those guys were your friends. How could you kill them?"

"Friends? Ha!" Aaron said. "Friends don't rape someone's girlfriend. I've hated you all since that night."

"So, you strangled Marty and hung him over the railing?" Cassie asked. The longer she kept him talking, the better. She had to figure a way out of there.

Aaron nodded proudly. "I went inside after you left the house and asked him why you'd been there. He wouldn't tell me. Said it was personal. And he was already drunk, so I had the upper hand. I strangled him with a cord from one of his small lamps and then found rope in the basement. Believe me, lifting his lifeless body over the railing wasn't easy."

Cassie covered her mouth with her hands. This was too much.

"And Tony?" Jason asked. "You shot him?"

"I did," Aaron said, smiling. "He was freaking out, worried that Cassie would come to his house. I asked him if he had a pistol for protection, and he showed me the gun in his desk drawer. I asked to see it, and that's when I shot him. He never saw it coming."

"Jesus, Aaron," Jason said under his breath.

"What about Craig?" Cassie asked. She moved a step closer to Jason. His firearm was still in his holster. If she could reach it while Aaron talked, she could use it to stop Aaron.

"I had to get creative with Craig," Aaron said. "He was so freaked out that day, and after you visited him that night, I stopped by to check on him. He already had a bottle of whiskey on his table and had drunk quite a lot. I got a shot glass and joined him. When he wasn't looking, I dropped a cyanide tablet in his whiskey. It was a messier death than I'd anticipated, so I had to clean everything up and set him back in his chair before leaving. But it did the job."

"Where did you get cyanide?" Cassie asked, backing up another step closer to Jason.

"You can get anything on the internet," Aaron said casually.

Cassie was scared out of her mind. Aaron was acting like killing the men had been a fun little adventure. She knew he was going to kill Jason next. If only she could get Jason's gun.

"It's finally your turn for revenge," Aaron said sweetly to Cassie. He drew closer to her and handed her the .22 pistol. "Shoot him, Cass. Blow his brains out for what he did to you. For everything they all did to you."

Cassie stared at the pistol in her hand. She could shoot Aaron instead and get Jason out of there. But if she missed, she could be the next one shot. Aaron still had his service revolver on his side, and the holster was unsnapped.

"Shoot him!" Jason yelled as if reading Cassie's mind. "Kill him. He's the monster."

Aaron glared at Jason. "I can't wait to see you dead," he said, his voice so evil chills ran up Cassie's spine.

Cassie stared between the two men. Jason was scum, but it wasn't up to her to kill him. Aaron was out of his mind, but she'd known him her entire life. She couldn't kill him. "No!" She threw the pistol across the room.

"Why?" Jason cried pitifully. "You could have saved us."

"I'm the only one who saves people," Aaron said angrily. "You kill them."

"Aaron," Cassie said gently. "No one has to die. We can all just walk away from here. I can go home and forget this ever happened. Jason can, too. Please, let us go."

Aaron shook his head. "No one's going home," he said. "I love you, Cassie. I proved I'd do anything for you. After Jason's dead and this place is burned to the ground, you and I will go away together. We'll be happy. Just like when we were younger. You've always been my best friend, and I've always loved you."

Cassie deflated. Aaron was delusional as well as insane. She knew then that she wasn't getting out of this unless Aaron was dead.

Aaron turned and walked into the other room, leaving Cassie alone with Jason. Quickly, she ran to Jason's side and unsnapped his holster.

"Hurry," Jason whispered.

Cassie grabbed the grip.

"What are you doing?" Aaron shouted, causing Cassie to pull away.

She turned to him. Aaron had a gasoline can in his hands. "I was just checking on Jason," she said, her voice trembling. "I'm a nurse, remember? I can't watch someone suffer."

Aaron narrowed his eyes. "You were trying to get his gun, weren't you. You were going to save him."

Cassie stepped back. "No. I promise I wasn't."

Aaron shook his head. "I thought you loved me, Cassie. But you'd choose your rapist over me?"

"No, Aaron. No. I do love you. I've always loved you," Cassie said. She knew she sounded desperate, but she'd say anything to get out of here alive.

Suddenly, Aaron started splashing gasoline all over the room. He poured it on Jason and all over the rug. "I'm going to burn this place down, and there won't be a trace of anyone when I'm done."

Cassie panicked. She glanced behind her and remembered she'd thrown the other gun back there. As Aaron sprayed gasoline everywhere, she backed up toward the pistol.

"You're insane!" Jason yelled at Aaron. "You'll never get away with this. Someone will figure out you killed me and track you down."

"I've had enough of you." Aaron pulled out his service pistol, walked up to Jason, and shot him in the head.

Cassie screamed. Scared out of her wits, she ran to the

other pistol and picked it up. She turned, only to see Aaron standing next to Jason's dead body, holding his firearm aimed steadily at her.

"Put it down, Cassie," he said calmly. "I'll give you one more chance to live. Leave with me, and we can be happy together. Otherwise, I'll have to kill you too."

The smell of gasoline permeated the room, making Cassie's stomach roll. She was closer to the door than Aaron. If she could just get outside, she could make a run for it. But before she could move, Aaron lunged at her. She sidestepped him, causing him to fall and hit the end table. The lit oil lamp sitting on it fell and broke.

Cassie screamed and moved back as the gasoline caught fire and roared to life. Flames jumped and danced before her, following the trail of gasoline Aaron had poured on the floor.

Aaron jumped up and tried to get away from the flames. His clothing was on fire.

"Cassie! Help me! Help me!" he screamed.

Cassie ran for the door with his screams in her ears. She turned and watched as the flames enveloped her childhood friend. Aaron sounded like a wounded animal, crying for help. There was nothing she could do for him, but she couldn't stand watching him suffer. With tears in her eyes, she lifted the pistol and shot him twice. Then she dropped it on the floor as Aaron dropped to the floor too.

Stepping backward, away from the heat of the flames, Cassie stared at the burning cabin. It was her nightmare all over again. Except that this time, she hadn't been saved. She'd saved herself.

Getting into her car, she drove away into the dark night.

EPILOGUE

Months Later

Cassie sat in the nurses' break room for a bite of lunch before a surge of new patients came into the ER. She picked at her salad as the nightly news played on the television in the corner. As she looked up, she saw a video of a flaming cabin, and her heart pumped wildly.

"Can you turn that up?" she asked the nurse closest to the control.

The woman hit the button, and Cassie listened as a Minnesota news reporter spoke.

"There are still no answers for investigators in Morgan Falls, MN, about the deaths of Sheriff Jason Hughes and Deputy Aaron Jackson in the burning cabin a few miles outside of town," the reporter said. "Also, the deaths of three men prior to the sheriff and deputy's deaths have yet to be solved. While the deaths all appeared to be suicides, the cases haven't been closed because the local coroner disagrees with that assumption. As in the case of Hughes and Jackson, both bodies had gunshot wounds to the head, making it appear it may have been a murder-suicide. Acting Sheriff Kevin Dudley states that the truth may never be known."

Cassie stared at the screen, wondering if she'd ever be tied to the burning cabin. No one had ever contacted her. She hoped it would stay that way.

"In other related news," the national anchorwoman said, "Due to an anonymous tip, two women who'd been missing twenty-two years and twenty-one years respectively, Tiffany Wexley, age nineteen, and Amanda Glass, age twenty, have been found in shallow graves on the same property outside of Morgan Falls, MN where the cabin burned down. There are no answers yet to how they ended up there or who killed them, but at least their parents will have closure."

"Isn't that the town where your mother lived?"

Cassie jumped and turned, then placed a hand over her heart. "You scared me to death," she said, forcing a laugh. Emily, her best friend from college and her co-worker stood there. "Yes. Same town I grew up in. But that happened after I left."

Emily sat down next to her. She knew Cassie's true story but not the names of her attackers. She was the one Cassie had sent the DNA samples to so they could be sent off to a facility there in San Diego.

"How was your son's first year of college?" Emily asked.

"He loves it. He's going to take summer school classes, too. He wants to get through his required classes quickly so he can move on to the classes he enjoys."

"He's a bright kid," Emily said. "Has he decided on a major yet?"

Cassie nodded. "He wants to study criminal justice as a

precursor to becoming a lawyer or working in law enforcement."

"Wow. Good for him," Emily said. She lowered her voice. "Did you ever find out who his father is?"

Cassie sighed. "I got the results, but I never opened them. I decided it didn't matter. Ryan is a good kid. Kind, sweet, smart. The only father he ever needs to know about is James."

Emily nodded. "I agree. You won the lottery with James."

"This will always be between us, right?" Cassie asked. "Even James can never know I got DNA samples from the men who attacked me."

"Of course," Emily said. She reached for Cassie's hand. "Best friends keep secrets forever."

Cassie smiled. It was finally over and behind her. Forever.

End

ABOUT THE AUTHOR

D. L. Sletten writes murder mysteries and psychological suspense novels. Sletten lives in Minnesota plotting books in a cabin in the woods.

D. L. Sletten's website: www.dlsletten.com